the stars at oktober bend

'An absolute tour de force! So beautifully written
and an unforgettable narrative "voice" this is definitely
one of the outstanding reads of the year so far'
- *Joy Court, School Librarian*

'It is incredibly powerful, haunting, spirited, joyous.
Like all of Millard's work, it is a story that makes
you feel. Don't let it pass you by.'
- *Melanie McGilloway,*
Library Mice blog at www.librarymice.com

'The Stars at Oktober Bend is poetic, startling and
intelligent, and comes with my heartfelt,
urgent recommendation.

It's most definitely one of my
favourite books of 2016'
- *Zoe Toft, www.playingbythebook.net*

the stars at oktober bend

GLENDA MILLARD

Old Barn
Books

First published in Australia and New Zealand in 2016
by Allen & Unwin
First published in the U.K. in 2016 by Old Barn Books Ltd
This updated edition published in 2017

www.oldbarnbooks.com

Copyright © Glenda Millard 2016

ISBN 978 1 910646 15 1

Ebook ISBN 978 1 910646 17 5

Cover and text design by Ruth Grüner
Title lettering by Joe Simmonds
Cover photos by Getty Images / iStockphoto

MIX
Paper from
responsible sources
FSC® C104608

FOR MUM
01/11/1924 – 18/07/2015

Special thanks to Sue Flockhart
for your patience, understanding
and for letting me fly.

G.M.

contents

there is no falling...
only flying... I rise...

1 ALICE

about forsaking and not

i am the girl manny loves. the girl who writes our story in the book of flying. i am alice.

they sewed me up when i was twelve. mended my broken head with fishbone stitches. tucked my frayed edges in. tucked everything in. things meant to be and things not. do it quick. stem the flow. stop life leaking out of alice. that's all that they wanted. so gram said.

broken alice. and forsaken. there was always forsaking in our family. first our father. then our mother, april – and after the stitching, our papa, old charlie, went too. only gram – grandma glorious – and joey stayed. brother joey, who said that love was at the bottom of all that forsaking. wrong love. love that hurt. he was ten when he said it. but older, much older. promised he'd never forsake me. and i believed him.

joey would have bled us both. nicked our finger-skins with old charlie's pocket-knife. smudged our blood together like we used to when we were little. when we made promises we thought we could keep. but joey couldn't cut me when i was number twelve. not even a little bit. not after what happened. he didn't have the guts to. instead he took tools from the shed. chisel, rasp and hammer. sharp he filed the chisel's blade. sharp enough to slit a lamb's throat. for weeks of afternoons he disappeared. chipped and chiselled in secret. showed me what he'd done when it was finished. wrote his promise for all the world to see. scraped it on the red gum that held up the bridge down on oktober bend.

joey and alice forever

between him and me he'd scratched a crooked heart.

then came bear and it was like the beginning of something new. no one ever came before. dear bear, constant companion, maremma, shepherd dog. strong, swift, silent bear. teeth and hearing sharp. wiring perfect. could have torn a man's throat out in seconds. would have. for me.

2 ALICE

plans a & b and the bee-wing book

plan a: joey would take me to school. to high school with him when i was mended. but there was too much noise and my electrics went haywire. there was no plan b. so i went home. was sent home. stayed home.

i remembered words, struggled to speak them. forgot how to arrange them. how to join them on a page. to begin with i wrote short things. lists and notes to self. some lines finished with a word that reminded me of what i wanted to say next.

school is loud too
many people
joey brings me
books teaches
me things looks
after me.

before manny came, before i saw his face or knew his name, before i touched his skin, i spent my days indoors. then bear beguiled me. waved her feathered tail and smiled and led me down sunlit paths. through our paradise garden. i tried to write about the things i saw. simple things.

ghost dog
sage spears
rosemary blue and new-minted
green
leaves

then gram thought of plan b. joey took me to the bus and i went to day centre. for two weeks i went. it was like school but worse and i came home. again.

we had books at home. quiet books that did not short-circuit my electricals. our dictionary lived on the mantel-piece. squeezed between the chimney bricks and canisters, tea-leaves, rice and sugar. gram's bible hid in her under-wear drawer, holy pages thin as bee-wings. joey said the little-lettered stories on them were only make-believe. like make-believe didn't count. but i loved gram's holy book for its gold-edged pages, strange words and mysteries. when joey forgot to bring proper books home from the library, i read the dictionary. or sometimes stole gram's bible from its tangled nest of petticoats and underpants. sneaked under the house with it and read aloud to bear.

once-upon-a-time there were two kings. one called david, the other solomon. the kings wrote poems. they were poet kings and the poems they wrote were called psalms.

their poems were recorded on the bee-wing pages. i used them to remind me of how to arrange my own words together. the poet kings wrote of wars and sheep and goats, lovers with nice teeth and red cheeks and someone called the lord. i wrote mostly about joey and bear. strange, old fashioned poems like this:

joey leads me beside the river
lets* me lie down in green paddocks and
brings library books home for me.
though i walk through charlotte's pass
i will fear no evil
for bear is with me
papa's gun is in the wash-house to protect me.
joey and bear will stay beside me
and we will live at oktober bend forever.

* note: the poet kings might have used 'makes' instead of 'lets'. but some words happen my heart to thunder in my chest. my electrics to hiss and fizz like wetted sherbet in my head. 'makes' is one of them. 'makes' and 'make' and 'made'. they remind me of when someone forces you to do something. in green paddocks or under the stars at oktober bend. or anywhere else. 'lets' gives you a choice.

3 ALICE

feathers for old charlie

joey's skinned knuckles gnarled over. his hammered finger-nails purpled and peeled. new ones grew pale as scalded almonds. other sores didn't heal. joey wouldn't let them. picked at the scabs. kept them raw so he wouldn't forget. scars to remind him like the message on the bridge.

my scars hid under hair grown long and curly as old mattress springs. strangers looked at my wild red locks and weed-green eyes. stared at my colours and curves. didn't know about invisible stitches or crazy circuits. didn't understand that my slow, unjoined speech began as perfect thoughts. hadn't heard of the curse cast upon me. the spell of twelveness.

only nearest and dearest knew that. it was family business. like the calm pills that snuffed out joy and sad-ness equally. balanced moods. made life flat. gram and joey saw the sideways shift of stranger's eyes when i spoke. watched blood rush to their cheeks when they figured out i was not what they expected. i didn't care what strangers thought. but i cared about gram and joey. so me and bear stayed mostly home.

when i grew braver, bear walked me to the river. under the swing bridge at charlotte's pass we went. out over the small bald hills through the black ironbark forest to places only me and bear, joey and old charlie knew about.

there i gathered the wild
flowers bright
billy buttons
bread and butter bush and
creeping purple
sarsaparilla
arranged them into jam jar posies for the sill above the sink.

but mostly i took feathers home. surprising gifts from the birds, floating, falling, free. i learnt the art of fly tying from papa charlie. while i searched for feathers, wool and other ingredients that i needed, i wore papa's canvas bag across my shoulder. striped orange, brown and white with moss green underneath. offcuts from gram's deck-chair.

the deck-chair satchel bulged with papa's tools:
a capstan ready-rubbed tobacco tin filled
with bright, sharp hooks
fine-pointed scissors
heavy-pointed scissors

clippers and a
dubbing needle a
sharpening stone and a book

the book was titled *fly tying: the definitive guide to hand tying flies for trout.*

in a pocket on the outside of the deck-chair bag was *my* book of flying. i kept the two books apart. it seemed wrong for them to touch. there were pictures inside papa's book i did not like. especially the one on page 44. i glued it to page 45 with flour-and-water paste. that way i could not see the picture by mistake if i was looking for how to tie a silver doctor or a muddle minnow. or reminding myself of the difference between a hair-wing coachman and a hair-wing *royal* coachman.

since then i have discovered the story of how the royal coachman came to be. a man named john hailey once made a coachman. but he added a little band of silk around the middle and a tail of wood duck feathers. someone, when they saw it said,

'here is a fly intended to be a coachman; but it is not the true coachman, what can you call it?'

'oh that's easy enough, call it the royal coachman for it is so finely dressed,' was the answer.*

* marbury. mary orvis *favourite flies and their histories* 1892.

8

old charlie knew the lures all by heart. learnt them from his father when he was number eight. but they did not let my papa charlie have scissors, hooks or dubbing needles in that little room without stars. in case he used them to rip the veins out of his wrists or damage his keepers. gram said that no allowances were made for an old man who committed a crime of passion.

i missed papa. missed all the things we did together. especially making flies.

joey said there was no reason why i should not make them. no reason why i shouldn't sell them to jack faulkner like our grandfather did.

i told myself all the reasons why i should.
to pay the debt
i owed old charlie and
because they were beautiful and because
i could and
then i told myself not to think
about page 44
and the two rainbow trout
bloodied red
gills and mouths kissing the air and
the shut-eyed man holding them
as though he cannot bear to look
at the terrible thing he has done.
told myself that if

that picture should spring
to mind like a hook
in my throat then
i must imagine the ghosts
of the fish
coming out of their mouths
and going back into the river
where they belong.

4 ALICE

alice's book of flying

begun by chance
by happy accident
on stolen pages
is less about
feathers or flies
or wings and more
about words
how they caught me
by surprise
raised me
in their rushing
updraft
lifted me
from pen and page
into the clear midair
gave me a bird's
eye view.

it was begun that one brave day when i emptied out my mediocre-making medicine.

flushed my calm pills away with toilet-water. then filled myself with fright that i had poisoned oceans and rivers. imagined fish, belly-up like capsized smiles. no more shimmering, swimming or cool blue dives. flushing was a risk i could not take again. from then i kept my pills in a cadbury's roses tin that smelled of a christmas past.

tinned pills set my thoughts loose. some pressed heavy on me. unspeakable questions of what did or did not happen when i was number twelve. unanswerable wonderings of what eternal twelveness meant and what might or might not happen in the ever after.

other thoughts lit like wings upon my shoulders. and because of them i one day wished aloud. said words for what i wanted. pens and inks, and clean white pages. joey brought them in the morning. jars tumbled from his emptied pockets down the blankety hills. lay there like jewels in the soft valley between my thighs while i stared jumble-headed in the earliness.

'pinched them from the newsagent.' joey's warm brother-breath curled like feathers in the cold air. 'made a speedy getaway.' he said and i, still dream-eyed, saw him on his bicycle, paper-stuffed shirt. jars clinking, legs pumping with fright and daring.

he sat beside me while i held the stolen colours up to the new morning light. one by one. the violet, the blue and the black. a book of empty pages lay open on my lap. a journey to be taken. was this what love looked like? stolen inks and empty pages? was it good love? in the quiet of the afterwards i wrote down a thing i thought. a small and simple thing. a gift for joey.

> if it's not love that makes you stay
> i set you free

i did not show the words to him. not then. not ever. on a stolen page i wrote them. a small step on a long path to learn the power of words. even my words. i named my book for what words gave me. alice's book of flying.

5 ALICE

communication strategies

oh patient book of flying! at first the words i put on paper came slow. not like the quick, careless voicewords i heard other people use. in my separateness i searched for fresh words and old forgotten ones. looked for them in the bee-wing book, the dictionary and in library books joey brought home for me. others i collected from the yarns gram spun. book of flying had no ears to judge me. what i wrote there was a conversation with myself.

but even i knew words are made for sharing. sometimes i wrote mine on scraps of paper and took them to the railway waiting room. offered them to passengers and passers-by. no one ever stopped, no one ever took a poem. i guessed they'd heard the stories of my madness and what had made me the way i am. or maybe it was old charlie they'd heard about.

'most people don't understand giving that's for free,' joey said. 'they probably think you want money or you're a religious freak or something.'

that's the way it was in the world outside oktober bend, he said, and i believed him. i couldn't remember what it was like before.

since no one would take what i wrote, i pinned it in places where people might stop and read. railway waiting rooms, fish-and-chip shops, church noticeboards and bus shelters. squeezed them between and under and beside lawn-mowing cards, lost and found notices and babysitting ads. sometimes i pasted speech bubbles on the paper lips of poster models. gave them words so they'd never be like me.

'in any language a scream is a scream and a smile is a smile.'

i even invented a word to describe the things i wrote. called them alicisms. i liked that word. it was mine.

in quiet corners, i pinned questions.

is love or flying the quickest way between two hearts?

is love or flying the most dangerous?

is love the only cause of forsaking?

i left spaces for answers and pencils tied to string and did not wonder if my odd questions were signs of shedding twelveness. the only responses were rude ones. until manny came.

6 ALICE

house of silence

once-upon-a-time we had a grandfather who lived with us and a telephone that did not work. joey said the phone company disconnected it because we didn't pay the bills. but that didn't stop gram shouting into the receiver when she got the debt collector's letters. she did it to fool us, joey said.

i don't remember gram shouting. that was before. i only remember after, when gram, joey, bear and me were all who were left. when gram was easier to say than grandma glorious. when i wrote lists instead of sentences and sounded like a tuba with a sock stuffed in its throat. when gram looked old and tired like other people's grandmothers.

after was when the landlord sent us an eviction letter. said the council wanted to demolish the house. told us we had to get out. out of our home. out of our place in the world.

'where will we go? what will happen to us if we don't?' i asked gram. 'will they put us in jail, like papa?'

'don't be stupid,' she snapped. 'we're not going any-where. we pay our rent, we got a right to be here.' from then on she burnt council letters and letters from our landlord in the stove. without even opening them. like that was going to save us.

joey was more practical. he cleaned old charlie's gun. oiled its two blue barrels. kept it ship-shape. and in spring when the rains came and the river rose, it was joey who dragged the boat out from under the house. tied it to a verandah post. safe as we could be. all of us. papa in the slammer. letters in the stove, gun under the house, boat on the verandah, companion constant, and secret at the angel's feet.

the secret appeared one morning in the earliness of my homecoming. body weak, stitching raw, thoughts unruly. but still i spied. spied it resting on the blue petals of a cloth daisy. thought i had found a little soul upon my sheet. pure as light, it was. clear and glistening. shapeless as a cloud. i cut around the flower. snip-snipped, careful as i could. hid it in a matchbox. the red-haired lady kept her heart-shaped lips closed. wouldn't tell. but i told joey. bothered him with questions he couldn't answer. bothered him to bury it. to his why i answered, 'in case it is the beginning or the ending of something precious.'

perhaps to please me, perhaps to end my botherings, dearest brother, gentle joey scratched a hole near the angel's stony feet. lay the matchbox there, covered it with sweet black soil and tufts of tender moss, he said. patted it down, snug and safe. a secret between him and me. a dear departed soul to keep teddy company. to this day i do not really know what was in the matchbox. perhaps it was filled with longing or with fear. or maybe with nothing at all.

for weeks afterwards, i wanted to ask joey to dig it up again. to make sure it was still there. scared it was or wasn't. scared it was part of my madness. only a dream. scared there might be loose ends after all. one thread pulled and i might come undone. so i said nothing.

months later, when a thread of fear fizzed like a lit wick, i wrote an antidote to fright in my book of flying.

we strange birds are safe
in our rust-chewed nest perched
on deep-driven bridge
piles on the mudflats of oktober
bend.

i was not the only one who left words unsaid. ours was a house of many silences. most of them left by the people who'd gone away: our father, sunny; and then april, our mother, who took her cello with her. papa charlie would have stayed, but they took him. made him go. he had no say in it. silence swelled with time. grew thick and heavy. not only because we couldn't hear the voices of our missing ones, but because sadness, hurt and anger made it too hard for us to talk about them. gram most of all. she ignored joey's questions like she ignored the demolition letters. and pretended she couldn't understand my slow, thick speech. days joey went to school, there was another silence. i learned to fill it by writing poems that nobody read. and questions no one answered.

7 ALICE

kith and kin

they don't let you receive phone calls when you're in jail. not even from kith and kin. but you can make them if the people you want to talk to have a phone that works. the only way we could talk to papa was to visit him. he didn't answer letters.

'how will we get there?' joey said.

'train,' answered gram.

'do you think you can make it up to the station?'

'i'll just have to, won't i.'

'we'll have to leave early then. leave plenty of time so's you can have a rest on the way.'

'i've done it plenty of times before.'

'before your lungs were stuffed.'

i wished joey would shut up. gram had never let us go with her before. she might change her mind if he didn't be quiet. but she ignored him.

'we'll go on sunday. children are allowed on sundays,'

gram said. she made me promise to take my tablets. 'and
if you don't feel too good, tell joey and he can take you
outside.'

the security people checked us to see if we had any contraband. all we had were explorer socks with extra-padded
soles, licorice allsorts, a fishing magazine and a poem.
i wanted to show papa how i could write now. wanted to
give him a clue that the doctors might have got it wrong. i
could not bring my lures to show him. we had to hand old
charlie's gifts over to security even though they were not
contraband. they promised us they would pass them on to
papa after we left. they let me sign my name on the poem
so he would know i wrote it.
    there were other people in the visitors' room when we
got there. men wearing green tracksuits talking to their
families. then they brought old charlie in. papa in a green
tracksuit. i never saw him in a tracksuit before. never ever.
least i don't think so. whenever i thought of him he was
wearing a flannelette shirt and khaki overalls. on visiting
sunday he looked shrunken down into his clothes. like a
turtle with its head pulled halfway into its shell. he smiled
when he saw us. didn't talk much. just kept smiling and
nodding his head. biting his lip. trying not to cry. i had my
pills inside me. chemicals hurtling round inside my veins.
i did not cry. i held papa's hand and my electrics hummed

smooth as summer honey through the wires in my brain. kith and kin we were. love made us strong. joey put coins into a machine and got us potato crisps and soft drink. i ate the crisps and listened to the others. did not say many things. did not want my voice to remind papa about what happened. about the reason he could not come home with us.

it was a long way from home to the jail where papa was. three hours to get there and three hours back. that is a long time for someone whose breathing apparatus is buggered. every time i asked gram when we could go again, she'd say,

'when my chest is better.'

when i asked joey if he and i could go by ourselves, he said,

'you've got to be eighteen to go without an accompany-ing adult. that's the rules,' he said. 'we go with gram or not at all.'

gram's bad chest meant that arrangements had to be made. she signed her name on a pile of green and white slips so joey could get her pension money out of the bank. joey and me talked about next of kin and what happens when you haven't got any who are not locked up. kin is family. kith and kin is friends and family. kindred is likeness. joey didn't count april as kin. didn't count our mother as anything. he never knew our daddy, sunny, and i couldn't remember much about him either. our daddy who is dead. our father who art in heaven.

some things we tried not to
think about like
what number gram was up to
and we shut our ears to her
strangled breath.
joey said so long as he turned eighteen before anything
happened to gram, we'd be okay.
if something happened before
no one need know
except us he said and
the small hill of green and white was
like a key
to gram's money.
joey never asked anyone
to the house or
talked about gram,
old charlie or me.
joey, bear and me were kith and kin, kindred. we were
everything to each other. that was before joey met tilda.
before manny came. tilda and manny were complications.
not even jack faulkner came to the house. gram wouldn't
allow it. the less that people knew about nightingale
business the better, she said. joey and me knew it wasn't
just the fly business she meant; it was personal stuff like

tar in her lungs,
eviction letters

old charlie behind bars
and me
not going to school.

meeting faulkner at the community centre was another one of gram's arrangements. made while she had breath enough to make them. faulkner lived in the city. came once a month on a thursday. after the country women's association meeting was over. gram volunteered to mop the floor. they gave her a key and she laid my trout flies on the kitchen table and let jack in the back door. when her emphysema got worse i took over the mopping. joey did the business. faulkner made out he was sorry for our gram.

'must be tough trying to raise two kids on the pension while her old man's in the slammer,' he said. he offered cash for my flies like he was doing us a favour. named a price. stuck out his right hand. hairy, gold-ringed pinky. but joey wouldn't shake.

'they're worth more than that and you know it!'

so faulkner said he'd pay more for flies made from rare feathers.

'it's damn good money for a retarded girl with no prospects,' he told joey. he never looked at me.

8 ALICE

on birthday number fifteen

i took things into my own hands. took the dictionary down from its place between the tea-leaves and the sugar. did some research into acquired brain injury and wrote my findings on the pages of the book of flying.

acquire v. gain possession of.

gain v. 1 obtain, esp. something desirable. 3 achieve
    7 reach (a desired place).

possess v. 1 have or own. 2 occupy or dominate the
    mind of (she's possessed of the devil).

be possessed of own, have.

desire n. 1 a feeling that one would get pleasure
    or satisfaction by obtaining or possessing
    something.

doctors say my brain has acquired, gained possession of, obtained or got, an injury. this much might or might not be true. the rest is incorrect. here are the facts:

- having a brain that does not work properly is not desirable. is not an achievement.
- i do not feel any pleasure or satisfaction in having a brain that does not work the way it should.
- there's no devil in there. just me and my thoughts hammering away at the walls. trying to break free.

dot point facts are
easy found, hard
to form
saywords come
slow and slurred
sound stupid
but heartwords fly
from my pen

the research part was easy. all i did was copy what someone else had written. non-fiction. stating my opinion took hours. finding the right words. arranging them on the page. when my work was done i wished there was someone i could show it to. someone who would read it and tell me it didn't look like a girl with crazy wiring had written it.

9 MANNY

Runaway

I am the running boy. The one who loves Alice. I am called Manny James.

The first time I saw Alice it was late at night and she was sitting on the roof of her house. You do not forget a thing like that.

The moon was big and bright that night and I was out running. Running is what I do when I cannot sleep. When I got to the footbridge over Charlotte's Pass, I stopped to catch my breath. The air was hot and still and I could hear a train in the distance. I looked down at the trees and bushes that grew between the railway and the river and that is where I saw a very strange thing.

It was a house on stilts I saw. I ran that way often, but I swear I never saw that house before. Way up high near the tree tops it was. Like it was floating there.

You must be dreaming, Manny James. Even in this land, houses do not float in the trees. That is what I was thinking when a light came on in a window, high up near the roof of that house. The window opened and a person stepped out onto a small balcony. It was a girl. Her hair was very long. Down to her waist it was. That is how I knew that person was a girl. She climbed onto the railing, and my heart was beating fast and loud. Almost as loud as the train. Not fast because I had been running, fast because that long-haired girl started crawling up the steep roof and because the ground was a long way down. But I did not shout at her. I did not call out, *be careful, girl!* I could not. My tongue was dry, like the leather tongue of a shoe and my chest was tight with air that could not escape. The train got closer and louder and I watched that girl climb higher.

When she safely reached the top, the air went quickly out of me and I was very glad. But then she stood up and again I was afraid. This time I thought that girl was going to jump. I know what it is like to have no hope. I have been that way.

'No! Don't do it. Don't!' I screamed at the top of my voice, but the train was much louder than me and that girl did not move. She looked like a carving on an old fashioned ship, sailing through the stars. That is what she looked like. The seconds ticked slowly, slowly. Then she threw her hands up, that girl did, and tiny fragments came drifting down all around her. In the place where I came from there is no snow, but I have seen it in the movies. That is what the falling pieces looked like. I did not know it then, but that girl was Alice and that is the picture of her that I keep in my head. That girl on the roof making snow fall in summer. It is a thing I will never forget. The train passed slowly between us. Its trucks carried grain, not people, and it did not stop at Bridgewater Station. At the far end of the platform the train began to move faster, and by the time it disappeared the roof of the house on Oktober Bend was empty.

10 MANNY

The First Poem

I found the first poem that night. It was very quiet, as if the train had taken all the sound in the world away with it. I raced across the shunting yards, past the empty goods sheds and the broken carriages all covered in graffiti. I did not know why I was running so fast. The train had gone, and the girl, and I could not find a way to get down to that house in the trees but still I kept running. I ran through the subway and up the steps to platform one, then I sat down on a wooden bench and wiped the sweat off my face and chest with my singlet. I looked at the medallion hanging around my neck. It was a gift from kind Louisa James. She said it was a charm.

'A charm is like good luck, Manny,' she said. 'It will keep you safe.' That is what she told me. It was a shock when she said that. I did not think there were things to be kept safe from in Australia. No one had told me what happened to the girl called Alice. I wore the charm every day but only to please Louisa James. You do not need a golden charm around your neck to bring luck. Luck brought me to Bull and Louisa James, and they gave me a home in the house of many windows. They gave me many other things also, but nothing or nobody can keep you safe all the time. Not a charm, not a person, not luck. Not anything. That is a fact.

When I had stopped thinking about luck, I stood up to leave and put my foot on the seat to tighten the laces on the running shoes that Bull and Louisa James had given to me. That is when I saw the poster that was on the noticeboard behind the seat. It had a picture of a pretty lady on it. She was drinking Coca-Cola and someone had written '*Read My Lips*' beside her mouth, which was open just enough to let the Coca-Cola in. Then I noticed that pretty lady also had something pinned to her hand. It was a piece of paper folded to look like a small fan. The pleats were tied with thread to stop them coming undone. I took the pin out of the lady's hand, unwound the thread and straightened the paper and then I saw that the fan was made from an emptied packet of flower seeds.

'Yates Blue Velvet pansies,' I read, 'shades of indigo, violet and midnight.' I had never heard of pansies. Flowers do not grow well where landmines are buried. I studied the picture on the packet and those flowers reminded me of the faces that I saw in my dreams. They had big frightened eyes and no mouths. I dropped the paper on the seat and picked up my singlet. I needed to run again. That was the feeling

I had inside me when I thought of the faces. But, before I ran, I saw that there was handwriting on the back of the flower packet. That is what stopped me from running.

desire
my desire is
to be
understood
my soul is filled
with songbirds
but when I open myself to
set them free
they shit
on my lips.
anon

It was a night for big surprises. First that girl making snow on the roof and then that small poem on the number one railway platform. I read that poem many times and many times it made me sad. Sad for Anon, who had songs that no one understood, and sad because I had no songs left inside me. I did not know if I had a soul, but if I did, I was sure there was nothing there worth letting out.

I took that poem home with me, to the house of many windows. I pulled the bedcovers back and lay down, but only long enough to leave the shape of me there. Every night

I did this for Louisa James to give her hope that I would one day learn to fit into her world. The moon transformed the floorboards into a shining sea and soon I fell asleep like an island in the middle of it.

That night was the first I did not dream of my homeland, Sierra Leone – of the things I had seen there, of the people I had left behind. Instead I dreamt of finding a way to the house in the treetops and that girl on the roof. That girl I would later learn was Alice.

11 ALICE

lamentation – an utterance of grief

i am the girl manny dreamed of. the silent voice that called him in his waking and his sleeping. i am the nightingale. i am alice and i have music as well as words.

no one could tell me how the music came to be. and i could not remember how long it had been there. was it since the beginning – me listening while i floated like a star on a string in my mother's warm dark sea? april, humming prettily to the mermaidenly being in her belly? maybe, maybe not. old charlie left his guitar and his mouth-organ under the bed. joey said they had to drag him away. our mother left joey and me in our beds, put her favourite child, her cello, in its velvet lined case in the aeroplane seat next to her. in my dreams i am velvet lined. and i am empty.

when i woke up with fishbone stitches in my head, the music was there. it landed like fairy-wrens. tiny round bodies, long straight tails. lone birds and couples or flocks of three. perched on electricity wires, some with tails up, others with tails down. and upside-down birds, hanging like acrobats on a high trapeze. crotchets and quavers, semi-quavers and demi-semi-quavers. beautiful names for beautiful sounds. i knew from where the wrens perched which notes they'd sing. drew them, beak to tail on the grey underneaths of empty cereal packets. and later, in the book of flying. the words came after. from where i do not know. perhaps they were gifts from the wrens. sent to comfort me, to fill the silences others had left.

songs: many-splendoured things made of words, music and mystery. the mystery was why the birds came to me. did they know me by name: alice the nightingale? bird-girl? had they seen me naked at the mirror, staring at my hills and valleys, the landscape of my body? did they know how i imagined my shoulder blades were wing buds? days i climbed onto the roof and dreamed of flying to canada, had the wrens watched me?

the ravens came later. scratched the sky with sorrows. chased the wrens away. brought no joy, no song, no dreams of flying.

there is a line on a map called the forty-ninth parallel. i have seen it for myself – in an atlas joey brought home from school. the forty-ninth parallel is where canada is. canada and our mother, april. i tore the page out and kept it. thought my mother might know what to do about my brokenness. about the mediocre pills. about why the birds came.

april played cello with the royal philharmonic orchestra

on the forty-ninth parallel and other faraway places. i knew
this only because i heard gram tell hattie fox.

hattie
ran the post office
wore a grey-lead
pencil behind her ear and
had ways
of finding out
could bore a hole
into your soul with
her ice-coloured eyes.

gram never flinched. told hattie that april was young and
talented. no one should stand in the way of her success,
gram said sternly. hattie was first to look away. she gave
gram her stamps, fiddled with the parcel string and talked
about the weather until we left. at home gram did not speak
of april. joey said that when i was in hospital, old charlie
tried to bring me back from my long, strange sleep with
promises of our mother's return.

'april will come,' he'd whispered, 'she always comes.'
april did not come. but old charlie's words trickled down
into the soft pink labyrinths of my unlistening ears. stayed
there till i was fifteen, when the want to remember rose
up like cool, green sap inside me. hard to know if what i
remembered was dreams or truth, wishes or lies. i never
dreamed about april. only the velvet lined case. dreamed

there had been a child there. was i the child or was the child mine?

i woke unafraid of falling. unafraid of stepping off the edge. the falling had been done. now there was only flying. joey wasn't afraid either but he was too heavy to fly. twelveness sometimes made things seem simpler than they really were. complicated when they weren't.

i once believed anger was the only thing that heavied my brother and old charlie, kept them earthbound. i wrote a poem for them. an utterance of grief. a lamentation.

> flying
> is letting go
> fury
> is a ball and chain
> what poor birds are we
> he won't fly and
> i can't sing and
> no one listens
> when a caged nightingale cries
> freedom.

poems mean whatever people want them to. that is why i like them.

12 ALICE

the comeuppance of jack faulkner

joey pinched a magazine with shining pages and photographs
of boats. he only took it to show me an advertisement for a
company called faulkner flies. there were coloured pictures
of lures –, my lures with information about each one. the
caption called them *collector's items*. joey said that meant
they'd never touch water. they'd be mounted and framed
and hung on walls in the homes of rich people, or stored in
purpose-made wooden boxes with brass hinges and clasps.
lures to catch people instead of fish. flies to be envied and
admired. i felt happy. no dead fish. no bleeding gills. then
joey said faulkner sold my flies for ten times the money he
paid us. he said it was time faulkner got his comeuppance.

some words disappeared from me altogether. leaked out
before the fishbone stitches mended me. comeuppance
must have been one of them. i had no idea what joey meant.
he pointed to the photographs of my lures.

'look at the labels they've made for your flies. they're

38

pretty ordinary. you could do better. you could draw pictures
too. why don't you make some before faulkner comes up
next time?'

at day centre they showed us how to make things like
paper, aprons and library bags. then they sold them to
people who could have made anything they wanted, but
didn't because they went to school and university and
got jobs and then there was no time left over for making
anything. i didn't go to day centre for very long because of
my crazy electrics. but i took my paper home and kept it
until joey said about making labels for faulkner.

i made my labels like tiny books
folded the paper
tore it careful
along the crease-marks
sewed pages
inside covers
with a needle gram used
to stitch roasting chickens after
she filled their emptied stomachs
with bread and thyme
egg and sage and onion.
inside each book i wrote
the name of the fly
its type
wet or dry

longtail matuka or parachute
opposite i listed what
feathers i used and where
they were found
whether the bindings were
linen or silk and
the weight and
the size
of the hook.

last of all, on the covers of all my tiny books, i wrote a fancy 'n' for nightingale and decorated it with drawings. pictures were easier for me to make than words. seemed to come from a different place in me. i made them look like the ones i'd seen in a book the priest gave to gram. i was in hospital when he brought it to the house, but joey was there. saw and heard it all. gram told him she didn't want his book.

said
she would rather
her granddaughter undamaged
her husband out of jail and
hoped the people responsible
would rot in hell
told the priest never
to set foot
in her house again
joey said the priest laid the book down

and when he was gone
gram threw it
after him
my heart is weighed down to
think of its twisted spine
crushed pages
words and pictures smothered
by the cold
hard floor.

joey saved the book. smoothed its pages, looked inside the cover where the priest had written words that riled our gram. the curly script was mysterious as the foreign language printed on its pages to a boy who was ten. but he kept the book. put it under the house with the gun that our grandfather hid before the police came.

later, much later, after i woke from my strange sleep. after they took me home and i learnt to trust bear, i followed her under the house where she kept bones, gumboots and tennis balls. there i found the unwanted gift wrapped in plastic, hanging from the ceiling in a string bag. it was called the book of kells. i thought it must be the most beautiful book in the world. the pictures inside were mostly of saints, animals and birds.

i thought of gram while i looked at them.
she, hollow as a roasting chicken

heart and soul and giblets
all torn out,
wished
i could persuade her to look
at the pictures,
thought
their wonderfulness might help
fill her
silences and spaces.

and when i finished making labels for my lures, i wished
i could show *them* to gram. did not want to be the cause
of her everlasting despair. wanted her to know that not all
of me was damaged. on the cover of every label where i
drew the 'n' for nightingale i disguised joey's head amongst
dragonflies and flowers, birds and feathers and fish. twined
them all together, tangled as dreams. coloured them with
inks i made from

berries, beets and bracken

onion skins and walnut shells

but dared not show gram what i'd done for fear she'd
guess we'd kept the book of kells.

when the inks were dry, i pressed the labels flat between
the dictionary's leaves till the next time joey went to the
country women's rooms. he said i didn't have to come. but
i wanted to. was curious to see faulkner's face when he

looked at my labels. when he got his comeuppance.

i stood with joey, opposite the man from the city.

'ah, the flymaker of bridgewater,' he said. his eyes
crawled over me.

i lifted my labels
from between the wordy pages
laid them flat on the table
watched him fill his lungs with smoke
and drop his stinking cigarette end
on the clean mopped floor
grind it
under his hard city sole
saw his arms spread wide
on the aluminium rim
of the pink laminex table
head hung low
between his shoulders
close to my labels
we stared
me at him and he at
my labels while
earth moved
tides turned
and the universe grew a little older
smoke leaked from
faulkner's nose spilled
from the corners of his mouth

curled upwards to
the ceiling like
the holy ghost and he
crossed himself and whispered
o sweet jesus

joey looked at me and said nothing. i kept my eyes on faulkner till he could no longer ignore the loud silence between us. he straightened his spine. tore his eyes from the labels. looked at me like he was trying to read a book with pictures but no words. i did not look away.

'holy shit, they're genius,' he hissed.

'yeah, they're genius all right, and they'll cost you fifteen bucks each, on top of the lures,' joey said.

before we went home joey took me to the newsagency, peeled off a note from the roll faulkner had paid him and bought me a small, square bottle of gold ink.

i never saw faulkner again. cannot remember
the colour of his eyes
the lines of his past
the shape of his lips
the pitch of his voice or
the smell of his money
but i cannot forget how both the sacred and the sinful slipped so easy from his tongue. light and dark together. fire and ice. i loved the way holy howled like a hymn up

the back of his throat, how shit hissed and spat like hail on
the fires of hell. perfect opposites. the one made the other
deeper, richer, more terrible and true.

later, much later
when manny and i found
one another when
we met and touched
skin and breath and soul
the only way we could
unpick the stitches
that locked our secrets inside
was to use words
the way faulkner did

13 ALICE

dove amongst the pie-wrappers

as though she knew that even wishes thought impossible sometimes come true. as though she knew about the boy on the bridge, bear woke me early. on the morning after manny james watched summer snow fall from my roof, she led me through the dewy garden, ducking apple-clustered branches. sunlight fingered scarlet runner beans, x-rayed peas in see-through pods. bear stopped at the fence behind the waiting rooms. sniffed the new sky, squeezed through a gap in the wire diamonds. and i followed.

as though she knew exactly where that boy had been: on the bridge, across the steel spaghetti in the shunting yards and onto platform one, bear led me.

the poster model gazed at me,
the girl who put words in her mouth,
i stared back
looking at her empty hand
looking for that missing thing i

lifted the gardener's notice
shifted the theatre royal program
checked the rubbish bin and between
the slats on seats where people pushed
brown paper pie bags
sat and stared
into the fairy-floss morning
giddy-minded with the
delicious mystery of who
had taken my words

i dipped into my bag. took a handful of papers on my lap. searched for something to fill a gap the size of the pansy-packet poem. took way too long. bear nudged me with her snout. i eyed the station clock, heard its ticking and its tocking. saw its narrow arm point to a dangerous black number. ten to departure time. bear trembled with faint sounds of faraway engines and wheels and footsteps of soon-to-come passengers. a distant runner jogged past the scout hall. i wanted to believe he was the night runner i'd seen on the bridge, small as a thumb in the moonlight. wanted to wait till he came close. to use saywords instead of written ones. to ask if he remembered a girl on a roof at oktober bend. wished for impossible things. that a few words of the poem i'd tossed into the night had found their way to the running boy. a fragment of me. a thought or two from my crazy brain.

bear's teeth tugged the hem of my skirt. i dared not let anyone see me with my bag of words. catch me in the act. anon, the girl with weird electrics. else my words might never be read. thoughts never shared. before the runner was close enough to see my face, bear and me vanished ourselves.

i did not see the poem escape my bag. drift like a feather. nestle like a dove in the litter and the weeds. did not see the running boy, straight as a spear, scan the noticeboard, in the pocket of his pants a poem tied with purple thread. bear and me were long gone when he found my fallen paper. smoothed it with his hands. sat and read my words.

i am
a rooftop poet
high on haiku
silently shouting
sonnets to the stars
giving wings to
words giving wings to me
together we fly
my milky-way words
and i

i did not know the runner was manny james. did not know my poem persuaded him that the person who wrote it, dropped it then vanished away, was the same girl he'd seen on the roof of the house at oktober bend. i did not know that wishes thought impossible sometimes come true.

ballerina on a bicycle

bear and me knew all
the detours
short cuts
hidey holes and how
to disappear
be safe

in seconds we were racing along the damp dirt track beside
the river. tiger-striped with sunlight and shadow. filled with
fruity air. my wires did not meander. my electricity ran in
straight black lines. no sparklers fizzed inside my head. no
clouds of ravens hovered. my eyes streamed, but only with
gladness. because someone had taken my words.

joey sat
unbuttoned
in the garden
crunching snow peas and

wearing rosella feathers and
fingers of light in his curls.
striped tie stuffed
in the pocket of his blue shirt ready
for school.

we flopped down beside him, bear and me.

'where've you been?' joey asked, and i opened my bag to show him.

'one gone!' i said. joey listened. heard excitement in my shapeless words. saw the salt marks on my cheeks. no one could protect me from tears. not all the time. not even joey. they happened mostly when my pills were in the cadbury's roses tin. not in me. i had not taken them that morning. gram woke before me. watched while i swallowed. asked me afterwards to open my mouth. prove its emptiness. i hid them well and now the tears came. joey's eyebrows worried themselves into a knot.

'did something happen?'

i shook my head.

'happy,' i said.

'good. i gotta go now or i'll be late again.'

we walked under the bridge and i pointed up at his carving.

'not forsaking?' i teased.

'nope. when i come back we'll go dancing. go home now. home bear, home.'

joey
was a garden-grower
day-dreamer
stone-skimmer
tree-climber
tune-whistler
fisherman
liar
and thief.

he did the shopping too and paid the bills. joey was not a dancer. but on wednesday afternoons he took me to ballet lessons. another activity someone thought would be good for a girl who might stay twelve until forever. joey rode his bicycle. my ballet shoes tied to the handlebars. me on the parcel rack behind him. bear was not allowed inside the scout hall unless she was muzzled. imagining bear with a cage on her face overloaded my electrics. muzzles were on the list with *make*, *makes* and *made*. reminded me of big hands and of not breathing. so on wednesdays bear stayed home under the house while joey took me dancing.

i put on the ballet slippers that the teacher, mrs cassidy, had loaned me. criss-crossed the wide satin ribbons. fastened them with loose loopy bows that drooped around my ankles. could not wear them tight. mrs cassidy always looked like she wanted to fix them. she never did. i think she was afraid of me. afraid of the falling down that sometimes happened. when i was ready, i sat on a long wooden bench by the wall. watched a girl whose face was a perfect oval. joey watched her too. her name was tilda. i should have known by the way he watched her, the way she danced ever closer to him, like a moth to a light, that she might become a complication.

tilda's hair was shiny as a raven's wing. she pulled it back, knotted it tight at the back of her head. wore three silver clips on each side and two at the back. her hair never moved. even when she leapt and spun not a strand escaped. it was truly magnificent ballerina hair. perfect hair, perfect face, perfect tilda. sometimes i imagined having hair like tilda's and dancing on the toes of my pink slippers. but mostly i didn't think about dancing at all. i let my thoughts meander. let myself feel sorry for tilda. none of her graceful movements sprang from joy, her smiles from gladness. even i knew that her kind of dancing was just a complicated kind of make-believe. planned in advance.

while i watched
perfect tilda,
i swayed to the music
ate furry peaches from a brown paper bag
traced initials
carved on the seat
fingered ancient chewing
gum underneath and

wondered
if the birds would come
hoped they would be wrens
not ravens.

tilda's dancing got better every week. things stayed much
the same for me. i didn't dance at all. not even a step. sometimes i ate cherries instead of peaches, or dangled them
from my ears. imagined me, dancing the flamenco and
writing birdsong on pure white pages. not at the same time.
but on the day manny rescued my poem from the weeds
something else happened. without warning.

bear was sleeping
in the shade
under the house
near the cadbury's roses tin and
joey was spellbound
by the hot, sweet scent of tilda
the grace of her arms
the tilt of her head.
he did not hear the young men's voices
did not feel the air move
did not see the shadow of the raven's wings
or smell the fear
bleeding out
of me.

15 ALICE

french knots and falling down

coach cassidy had brought the bridgewater bombers to the scout hall for pre-season football training. his wife, mrs cassidy, was going to help them with their stretching out, limbering up and flexibility.

the bombers were on the grass and on the porch and on the hard hot gravel. waiting for the dancing to stop. for the music to end. their voices bombarded the windows. bounced off the walls. rattled me.

the ribbons around my ankles grew tighter and tighter as i tugged, tried frantically to untie them. i wanted to shout,

let's go, joey!

wanted to scream at mrs cassidy that dancing does not fix your electrics.

but panic was huge and hot
a hand across my mouth and nose,
clouds of ravens
beat their wings
blocked the light

stole my air and i
slow-spiraled like
a dying swan.

a patch of grass. a bicycle shed. joey crouching. this is what i
saw when i came back with arms and legs and eyes all heavy.
stroke after slow stroke, joey wiped my forehead with something cool and damp. afternoon was thick with sunlight.
quiet now. dancers disappeared. footballers limbering up.
inside all but one. my eyes opened quick and wide to see
that last one. that one standing like my brother's shadow.

carved from ebony
polished with beeswax
a saint from the book of kells
a warrior
a dream with
embroidered-on hair
neat tight french knots
i wanted to
touch them
read them like braille
run my fingers along
the lumpy scar that joined
shoulder to elbow.
i wanted to

know why it was there
what had shaped this boy?

the coach put his head around the door and yelled, 'move it, jamesy!'

then i knew i was back from wherever i'd been. the boy in front of me was real and true.

joey held a wet handkerchief towards him.

'she'll be okay now, thanks,' he said, but the boy didn't seem to hear joey or the coach. ignored the handkerchief. stared at me. my hands crept to my skirt but joey had fixed everything. arranged my legs straight and together, tugged my skirt down over my thighs. like he always did when i was away. i made myself look into the other boy's eyes.

don't be scared, beautiful boy. please don't be scared. i was born normal and i'm still mostly normal. and anyway, it wasn't my fault. they warn you about everything else – don't take lollies from strangers, don't get in cars with people you don't know. but they never tell you why not. no one ever said don't watch the stars at oktober bend, little alice nightingale. no one told me there were people who did things like that to children. now my electrics are wrecked and my words come out weird and doctors say i might stay twelve until forever. maybe that's what my mother thinks. alice will still be twelve when she gets back. i can't know for sure, but i think i'm pretty much as fifteen as anyone else. and joey says that someday someone

will invent a way to fix my crazy wiring. till then i guess i'll
put my words on paper. but for a boy like you, i'd take my
mediocre pills. if that's what you want, i thought, *if that's*
what you want.

the cicadas kept up their racket. the coach hollered again
and the boy left. i did not know he was the boy i'd seen,
small as a thumb in the middle of the night and in the early
morning. the running boy.

    manny james following my paper trail. each poem bring-
ing him one step closer to finding anon. finding me.

    a hand touched my face. i looked at my wet fingers and
felt despair leaking quietly all over my cheeks. i took the
blue handkerchief from joey. sopped my sadness on its red-
and-white border and wondered where and who and why.

    where had the boy come from
    who was he and
    why had the coach called him jamesy when
    there was a red 'e'
    stitched on the corner of his handkerchief?

i pushed it into the toe of my dancing shoe. joey took my
hand.

    'let's go home,' he said.

    he wheeled his bike. i dawdled beside him. still not
quite right. but already thoughts of my falling-down faded
in the bright memory of the boy.

'don't tell gram,' i said when we were nearly at hattie fox's post office. i didn't want her going on about the pills i never took. joey nodded. we wouldn't tell her about the boy either. gram was suspicious or superstitious. or both. especially of anyone who was good looking. once she told me a story about an angel called lucifer, which means light. lucifer did something he shouldn't have. something so awful he was banished from heaven and transformed into a devil. prince of darkness was his devil name. he could masquerade as anything or anyone and ordinary people were fooled because he was so beautiful. i didn't want to be like gram. scared, suspicious, superstitious.

could the dark prince make himself look like a black boy with french knots on his head? i asked myself.

by the time we passed the post office i decided i didn't care.

16 ALICE

bargaining with the god
of flying things

bear met us at the chainlink fence. inhaled the smell of
stale fright from my skin and clothes. if she'd been allowed
to sit on the steps at the scout hall, she would have known
what was going to happen before it did. if mrs cassidy had
let her lie at my feet, i might have held her till she drove
the birds away. bear and me were more than kin or kindred.
spoke a language of our own. i put my arms around her. let
her lick my hands and face till my wires lay slack as cooked
spaghetti. untangled, loose. then she led us down the steep
embankment to the river track and home.

gram was dozing in old charlie's hammock, painted by
the red-gold afternoon. shadows gathered in her gullies and
folds. hair soft as dandelion fluff. arms folded like a kiss
across her apron. once as tough as any man's

they swung an axe
shovelled river loam

patched up our falling-down house
dragged old charlie away
from trouble
from the pub
home
arms gentled by love
gathered us in
told us when
our daddy was dead and when
our mother was gone
tough and tender arms
carried me home
broken and bloody
under the stars.

'everlasting arms,' i said softly, 'leaning on the everlasting
arms.'

lines of a hymn. gram had one for every occasion. did she
sing when she carried me home? i don't remember much of
that night. don't want to.

the best of it
a sky-full of stars
bright as new fish hooks
old charlie and joey
down on oktober bend
baiting shrimp nets.
the worst of it

> hands coming down
> over my face
> screams
> i couldn't scream,
> breath
> i couldn't take and,
> afterwards,
> the rock coming
> down and
> down and
> down.

'hurry up. get your things,' joey said.

on our way through the orchard we jammed our pockets full of hot blue plums. seven o'clock, daylight saving time and still scorching. crickets sang, cicadas shrilled. bear led the way. shrubs crowded the banks, alive with wrens and finches and firetails. we stopped at a fallen tree that spanned the river. joey baited a hook, tied a teaspoon-shaped sinker to the line and cast it across the water's tight grey skin. the reel spun, the float bobbed. joey planted the cork handle of his rod in the mud. swallows skimmed. caught gnats and mosquitoes. and i watched it all and willed the shy kingfisher to come.

sometimes while joey fished, i read *fly tying: the definitive guide to hand tying flies for trout* or wrote things in my own book. imagined wings i could have made from all the feathers i'd ever found. saw myself standing on the roof with them fixed to my shoulders, words and wings. it makes no difference. in my mind i am stepping off. there is no falling. only flying. i rise. born again. made new.

but this time, this airy evening, i was not seduced to fly. my body was anchored firm to earth by want to see the boy again. i chanted quiet charms and incantations. lips moving like a mad thing's. stealthy as night falls, i stole a bright hook from joey's tackle box. swift as a breath i pressed its barb to my wrist. closed my eyes and tugged. a bright bead of blood welled up. a ruby jewel. a sacrifice. a gift for the god of feathered things. i begged him bring the sacred kingfisher, bring down a shimmering feather. vowed i'd use it to create the finest lure ever made. a pretty thing to bring the broidery boy to me.

and when he comes
i will
pass to him
new poems
on fine white pages,
sonnets and songs
rows of notes
for words to waltz to
and when he reads them he will
know that i am
more
than twelve

more
than broken much
more
he will take
my hand press my fingers
gently into his
scarred places and i
will know their meaning.

the spell was cast, the pact was made. blood was the scarlet
seal on the witch's wrist. then joey spied the question mark
in my hand, snatched the hook. sucked the pretty beads
from my skin. pulled me rough, held me tight against his
chest.

'no more blood, alice,' he said. 'no more!' he dreamed of
blood, he said. of my face after the rock split my skull open.
'no more blood.'

that night the crickets sang love songs in earth's cool dark.
and i wrote an introduction to the boy i had bargained for.

for some
twelve is a nice number
but i
am alice
fifteen times
over

17 MANNY

Finding that Girl who made Snow on the Roof

I remember thinking, when I saw her lying there, that her hair was red as fire and her skin was pale as bone. I watched the boy straighten her skirt and make sure that her underclothing did not show. I saw how gently he stroked her arms and hair while her body jerked and twitched. His voice was calm and quiet when he spoke to her but he seemed angry with everyone else.

'Piss off, you bloody morons!' That is what he said. I was not exactly sure what these words meant, but it was clear he loved that girl.

When she woke up, the girl did not speak. But when she looked at me, her eyes and her quietness reminded me of other faces. Those faces were sad faces. Their eyes were very full because they had seen many things, but their lips could not be opened to speak of what they had seen. These were faces that followed me from the other side of the world because I had done nothing to help them. When I looked at that girl I wondered what she had seen that made her eyes so full. And I wondered if her lips, also, could not be opened to speak of those things.

Then I looked at the boy who loved her and I knew that girl was different from the people in my dreams. It was because of that boy she was different. That boy was not like me. He would not run away. That is what I was thinking while I watched them outside the scout hall.

That morning when I was running, I saw a girl and a dog in the distance. This girl, lying on the small green hill, did not have a dog. But they both had long hair and so did the girl on the roof in the night. Was it the same person? Was this bright-haired girl the one who made it snow in summer? Did she write the poem on the pansy packet? Was she leaving the poems for me? These are the questions that I asked myself and with all my heart I hoped she was that girl. I wanted to ask her the meaning of her poems. I did not know then that she would tell me that a poem can mean whatever your heart wants it to.

When the coach called to me, I became a shadow. It was a long time since I had shadowed anyone, but I had not forgotten how to. I walked close to the coach. Very close I walked, so that he could feel me like a cloak around his shoulders and he could see me from the corner of his eye. He knew that I was there. Then, when he walked back into the hall, I slipped away. There in the room surrounded by all those other boys, he would not have noticed that I was gone. That is how it is with a shadow. There it is, as close as a brother, as close as skin. So close that you forget to pay attention and then it disappears. That is what happens. That is what happened to Coach Cassidy. I was with him and then I was not.

I ran in the direction the boy had gone when he led the girl away. Behind the railway station waiting room and across the shunting yards, that is where they went. Just like that morning when the girl and her dog disappeared. On the other side of the shunting yards was a tall wire fence. It was covered with creeping plants and fist-sized blue flowers and I could not find an opening. Voices came to me from somewhere on the other side. I listened carefully to hear which direction they were coming from and then I climbed the fence, dropped quietly to the ground on the other side and took off my shoes and socks. That is when I became a shadow again. A shadow has no substance. It makes no sound. Leaves do not rustle when a shadow passes by and the tall grass does not bend. A shadow leaves no footsteps. In Sierra Leone the soldiers said that small boys make good shadows.

I looked and listened. It was easy to find them. The river and the birds helped me. The river carried their voices to me and when I looked down towards the place where the sound came from, tiny birds flew out from the tops of the bushes.

That is what birds do when someone comes near. Even if a shadow falls across them, they fly. Small birds watch the ground for the shadows of birds of prey. The yellow dog was not looking for shadows. I kept downwind where *she* could not catch my scent.

I crept through clumps of pampas grass. The feathery plumes were taller than I was. I could not see the river but I could smell it and I could feel damp, cool air rising up from the earth. Rivers everywhere have a way of doing that, a way of telling you where they are.

I found a place at the edge of the pampas grass from where I could see the river. Where I could watch them, that boy and that girl from the scout hall. I was thinking about the small green hill and the girl's hair and her sad eyes when I saw the boy take her in his arms. He did not put them gently around her, did not touch her kindly, carefully, the way he did at the scout hall. He moved suddenly as though he wanted to prevent her from doing something. I heard his voice rise but I could not hear what he said. Perhaps he was angry. The muscles in my legs grew tight with wanting to run. But the girl did not struggle. She leaned her head on the boy's shoulder, put it there herself. It was a puzzling thing for me to see, a boy who did not know they were family, who did not know their secrets and sorrows. I knew what I saw and that is all.

I felt the poems in my pocket. I did not need to read them. I knew the words by heart. And in my heart I was sure that girl had written them. A girl like that did not need someone like me. I should have left her alone with that other boy, but instead I curled up in my hiding place. I was very tired of running away.

18 ALICE

speaking to the dead

prayers or pacts or promises to
the god of flying things
blood and bleeding
changed nothing
changed everything
changed me
planted in me
a seed of knowing that i
even i could make
things happen.

so small, that seed, that i did not feel manny's eyes upon
me. did not expect him to come so soon. or at all.

a fortnight of slow days dawdled by, yet no kingfisher's
feather fell from the heavenlies. march arrived and with
it grew the feeling that blood and promises brought. the
knowing. something in the universe had shifted. a universe

so big and mysterious not even joey could explain it to me properly. the feeling was not new. i'd had it before. but never about kingfisher feathers or black boys. knowing filled me with fright but at the same time, made me feel safe. tiny and powerful i was. and light, light enough to fly. like my bones were hollow as a bird's. as an angel's.

joey wouldn't listen when i tried to explain *knowing* to him. he only believed in what could be proved. maybe that was why he stole things. put himself in danger of being caught to give me what i wanted. proof he loved me. or did he think that *knowing* was an odd belief, like unicorns, fairies and true love, that girls grew out of. other girls.

while joey was at school i went to talk to teddy about things known but not seen. teddy's place was fifteen minutes west of our house. halfway up the cutting near charlotte's pass. above it, the coin-in-the-slot barbecue. in the river below it was the tarpit, where the water was black as pitch to hide its secrets. deep as hell. bottomless, they said. no place for bones to rest.

a fancy metal fence surrounded teddy's grave. reminded me of an old fashioned cot i'd seen in a photograph of baby gram. a stern stone angel stood at one end of teddy's cot. stared at the scroll between her grey feet as if her blind eyes could read the words carved there.

here lies

edward (teddy) english

chosen son of the reverend and mrs lillian english

leaning on the everlasting arms

18 Dec 1907 – 1 Nov 1914

i wondered if lillian english held her boy that morning, that first day of everlasting loss?

once
i envied teddy
safe in the everlasting arms
while *i* tried
to remember
how to sleep
how to speak
how to write
when to take my pills and
what it was like
before
trying to forget
other things.

no one could hurt teddy now. but we nightingales kept old charlie's gun under the house. were shadowed by bear and thoughts of our past.

teddy seemed almost like kith and kin to me, like kindred. the tarpit and what happened there couldn't keep me away. i stepped over the low fence and sat on the edge of his forever bed. i spoke aloud to him of pacts and promises, of boys and knowing. teddy had stuttered, they said, so i was sure his ghost would understand my slurred and stumbling speech. while i talked i scraped lichen from the angel's feet, washed her face with the hem of my dress. crowned her hard grey hair with wildflowers and when there was nothing more to be said about knowing, reminded teddy about our secret.

'do you remember, teddy?' i said, 'you *must* – remember when joey scraped the dirt out from under the angel's feet? that's where it's hid, where no one else can find it. no one can take it away from me. never again. it's the best thing i ever gave anyone, teddy. better than all the nightingale labels put together. better than the book of kells. it squeezes my heart to leave it in the ground. but we didn't know what else to do.'

before i left i kissed the angel's feet and asked her to watch over us all, those on earth and those under the earth or wherever else they might be. when i stood up her cheeks were as pink as a pigeon's feet and the paper daisies in her crown shone like gold. you might think my electrics went crazy. you can think what you like but i swear it's true.

the legend of teddy english

from teddy's grave, there was a clear view of the tarpit.
down the cutting to the sheer rock walls. it was a lonely
place.

windless
soundless
no children's voices
no bird songs
rope thick as
a baby's arm hung
from a river
red gum
unmoved except
on hot nights when
boys came
drank beer
smoked
cigarettes and launched themselves off
the rope into

the still black
into the pit.

no one used the concrete block barbecue at the top.
travelling fruit-pickers sometimes stayed a night. rolled out
their swags and left again in the morning. families never
came.

i was a water baby. swam before i walked, first in the
warm dark sea of april. after in the sparkle and glimmer of
oktober bend.

because of my twelveness
short-circuiting electricals and powerful
imagination
i sometimes believed or
wanted to
my mother was a mermaiden
and i
a child of mer then
and now a mermaiden
wondering if the smear
on my sheets might have grown
into some sparkling thing
a soul with fins.

but for all that, i was afraid to think of water with no
end. even oceans and seas had floors and shores, could be
measured.

i was not disturbed by
the legend of teddy english
which might or might not be true because
that is the nature of legends.
or by the story
that the rope sometimes swung
by itself,
to didgeridoo
a dirge
for a boy who died trying
to do what no one else had,
touch the bottom
of the tarpit.
teddy was
that boy
they made of him
a hero
to hide
the shame of
fathers and grandfathers
teenaged when teddy fell
like a leaf from the tree.

old charlie's dad was there when it happened. said teddy
was bullied because he stammered. teased because his
daddy's skin was white as teddy's was black. teddy did as
they told him – to escape his misery one way or another. let

the other kids fasten a potato sack filled with river stones to his back.

'dad told us teddy was just a little fella,' old charlie said, 'too short to reach the rope, and the sack of rocks on his back was so heavy he couldn't climb the tree. so the bastards towed the rope ashore and heaved teddy up on their shoulders so he could reach it. he twined his arms and legs around it and he clung there scared out of his wits while they pushed him. singing out to him, they was, eggin' him on, dad said.

'dive, dive, dive! like that they went. but the little feller was too scared to let go and they got sick of waitin' and left him hangin' there while they got stuck into the home-brew. swiggin' it outta sauce bottles they was.

'me old dad was there and he swore it was true. he was only seven or eight at the time but he seen it all with his own eyes. him and teddy was mates. dad ran all the way to town but by the time he convinced the coppers to come back with him it was too late. teddy never cried out, dad said. from the top of the ridge they seen him drop into the water, quiet as a pin, and the water closed over him smooth as his mother's silk nighty. dad never forgot. broke his heart it did. poor little begger. teddy weren't no hero. the bastards just said he was so they wouldn't feel so guilty about what they done to him.'

papa charlie was a good storyteller. teddy's was a hand-me-down tale. one not written with pen on paper. but i remembered it ever after. word for word it's in my head. old charlie's telling of it.

teddy was never seen again, never found. there were no bones, no remains. nothing at all of him in the grave on the hillside. it was an empty memorial. only his spirit was there. i feel the cold on my arms and on the walls of my heart when i sit with him.

20 ALICE

down to the river

joey hated me going anywhere near teddy's grave. gram said the site was cursed. after i talked with teddy and the angel, bear and me walked to the fence that separated us nightingales from the rest of bridgewater. we waited there for joey.

and when he came
i didn't tell him
where i'd been or mention
the quiet excitement
the feeling
building
in me
didn't say anything
to make joey mad anything
about my wager with the god of feathered things.

i nodded when he said,
'feel like a swim?'

'you and me goin' down to the river, down to the river,'
i half hummed, half sang in my broken voice. 'you and me
goin' down to the river to wash our sins away.'

'don't sing that bullshit,' joey said, 'you've got nothin'
to wash away.'

he was serious too often. got mad too quick. maybe he
was always that way. maybe not. he might have changed
because of what happened. to me. and to all of us – because
of me. sometimes i thought joey and gram were more
messed up than me. our family history was a game of dom-
inoes played with people instead of tiles.

our daddy
sunny jim
toppled first,
too much drink
too many pills
not enough sleep and
a runaway road train.

then april, our mother, went looking for something else
to hold her up. left joey and me behind. we might have
been okay, just the four of us: joey, gram, old charlie and
me. but then i fell and old charlie grabbed the snake gun,
waited under the bridge. emptied both barrels into the
windscreen of the stolen ute. sent it somersaulting through
the starstruck sky. he paid with everything that mattered.
his family and freedom.

and gram
got eaten up
from inside out
by grief
arthritis and
nicotine.

joey was the last man standing and he was only fourteen.

i grabbed my brother's hand and ran. tugged him away from
his blues. twelveness is not all bad. at twelve you still play.
under the bridge we went. under our names and under
the crooked heart. i peeled off my dress, tossed it onto the
bulrushes and threw myself into the river.

21 MANNY

The Boy Who Loved Dares

Every week on Wednesday I went to football training early. And every week when the dancing girls came out of the hall and the footballers went in, I felt a girl watching me. She was small and neat with shining black hair. Other boys liked to look at her but I kept my eyes down. I wished that poetry girl would walk through the door. That is what I wished. But she did not come.

Louisa James says summers are always long and hot in Bridgewater. But my first summer in that place was very hot. In the second half of March the temperatures broke all of the records. That is how hot it was. After football training one afternoon, the other boys said they were going to swim at a place they called the Tarpit. I had heard of that place before but I had not been there. I thought it was a very strange name to call a place where people went swimming. I did not really want to go with them. But because it was very hot, I said that I would.

All of us footballers were jogging along the footpath in Kennedy Street when a person came from behind and started running beside me. I turned my head to look and saw that girl with shining black hair and she was looking back at me.

'Hi,' she said. 'Are you going to the Tarpit?'

'Yes, I am going,' I answered her. Then I did not know what else to say. There were two boys running in front of me. One of them was our captain, Lucas Stewart. The other one was Hamish O'Leary. I stared straight ahead at Hamish O'Leary. There was black dagger tattooed between his shoulder-blades and three drops falling from its tip. I wondered why anyone would want a picture of such a thing between their shoulder-blades. A bird of paradise or an eagle would have been better. This is what i was thinking when Hamish swung around. He ran backwards and smiled at that girl who was running next to me.

'Checking out my body art, eh babe?' he said to her although I do not think she had been looking at his dagger.

She did not answer his question but he just laughed and said, 'One day I'll get a tatt of your name, sweetheart. Just deciding the best place to put it. Close to me heart or lower down? Waddya reckon, babe?'

'You wouldn't dare,' she said carelessly.

It was not a smart thing to say to a boy like O'Leary. I wondered if the girl knew that here was a boy who loved dares. He laughed and sprinted ahead. I looked at the girl and I saw that pieces of her hair were coming loose from her silver clips and her cheeks had become dark pink. She slowed down and I thought that she might leave us. But she did not and I stayed with her. I could not run away.

'He's scum, that O'Leary,' she said.

I did not answer. I wondered what she would think of me if she knew about the things that I had done.

'I'm Tilda Cassidy,' she said, 'Lucas Stewart is my step-brother.'

'My name is Manny James.'

'I know who you are,' she said, 'everyone does.'

She was wrong. No one knew who I really was but I did not tell her that.

'I sometimes see you after dancing,' Tilda said. 'You know, outside the hall. I was there that day the girl had a seizure.'

We entered the subway under the railway tracks. It stank of piss and damp and other things that people do in dark places.

'She does not come anymore,' I said softly. I did not mean to say the words at all. I ran faster then. I hoped that girl called Tilda had not heard me. Just before we reached the other end of the subway, she reached out and grabbed my hand. Then she stopped running and held tight as though she was afraid that I would leave her. I did not want to stay in the subway and I did not want to hear what she might say. I looked at her hand and I saw that it was very small and mine was very large. I tried to meet her eyes and that is when I saw the writing on the wall behind her. It was not like the writing and pictures that I had seen on railway sheds and broken carriages. This writing was arranged in neat rows. It looked like writing I had seen before. I wanted to pull Tilda out of the way so that I could read it.

'I know,' said Tilda softly and for a short moment I did not understand what she meant. 'It's because my...the teacher thinks Alice disturbs the class. That's kind of why I wanted to talk to you.'

'Alice?'

'Alice Nightingale.'

Tilda still held my hand, but I did not feel it there. My thoughts were all of that girl on the small green hill outside the scout hall. That girl I had seen by the river and on the roof. The one called Alice. Alice. It was the first time I had heard her name, the first time I had spoken it. Her words were on the wall, her name was in my ears and on my tongue. Alice. Alice Nightingale. In another time, another place, there were nightingales in my life. Small, plain, brown birds with voices you would give anything to hear. But when war came, the birds left. Bull and Louisa James had given me a new life. They gave me food and shelter, an education and a chance to forget the past. There were some things that I did not want to forget. But now there was Alice and I wondered if I might once again hear a nightingale sing. This is what I was thinking while I was standing in the subway under the Bridgewater railway station and that girl called Tilda was holding my hand.

'Manny,' Tilda said, 'I want you to find out where Joey and Alice live.'

'Joey?'

Tilda nodded.

'Alice's brother. The boy who took her to dancing, who was with her when—'

'He is her brother?'

'Yeah, what did you think?'

I shrugged my shoulders. I could not begin to tell her all the things I had thought.

'Someone's coming,' she said. 'Let's go, it might be Lucas or O'Leary.'

Tilda let my hand go and we ran towards the exit. A man and a small boy on a green tandem bicycle rode in as we burst out into the light. There was a big orange pumpkin and a bunch of flowers in a basket on the handlebars of the bicycle and the air smelt clean and hot. That man was whistling like a bird.

22 MANNY

Tilda and the Tarpit

The Tarpit was a deep pool in the river. That is all it was, a swimming hole below the picnic ground. When we arrived some of the boys were already swimming in the black water and others were swinging on a rope that was fastened to a tree beside it. Hamish O'Leary was not in the water. He had taken all his clothes off and stood with his back towards Tilda and me. I saw the dagger and the drops of blood.

'You should go now,' I said to Tilda. 'This is not a good place for a girl to be.'

Hamish looked over his shoulder at us. Perhaps he heard me speak. He said something to Lucas and the others and made a crude gesture. It was not something you would want your sister to see. But Lucas and his friends all laughed.

'Go now,' I said again to Tilda, afraid of what Hamish O'Leary might do next. He did not know how to behave in front of that small neat girl.

'You haven't told me if you'll do what I asked,' Tilda said.

I did not need reminding.

87

'Please, Manny, I've only lived here since Dad married Lucas's mother, so I don't know that many people here yet. Everyone seems to know my step-brother and he seems to know just about everyone else.

'Why don't you ask him about Joey Nightingale, then?'

'I don't want him to know. That's why I asked you. You're different to Lucas and his friends.'

'What makes you think I am different?'

'Well, for starters, none of Lucas's friends would have told me to go home from here.'

I could have told her that the Nightingale's house was hidden in the bush only a few minutes away from where we stood. But then she might ask me how I knew. I could not tell her that I had followed them home. What would she think of me if she knew I had hidden and watched them?

And even if I had not done these things, all I knew about that small neat girl was that her father was a policeman and the coach of our football team, her step-brother was the captain and her step-mother was a ballet teacher. There were many other things that I did not know about her. For all I knew she might be like Bull James who gave me a name and a family and told me that someday I could have a house like his.

'There's nothing you can't have. It's simply a matter of choice and hard work.' That is what Bull said.

I could not tell him that no amount of hard work

88

could give me the things I would have chosen: my family, my country, peace. These were the things I dreamed of. I wondered what Alice and Joey dreamed of. They seemed different to all the other people that I had met since I came to Bridgewater. I could not tell what it was that made them seem that way. Their house was old and falling down but they had each other and their wild garden. Perhaps that was what they wanted, all they dreamed of. Perhaps, like me, they did not want a house of windows. That was something I could understand, but would Tilda?

Hamish and Lucas were almost at the water's edge and the others were running after them.

'Why do you want to know where they live?' I asked Tilda.

'I just – please Manny, say you'll do it for me.'

The air was hot and still. I needed more time to think. Tilda's step-brother swung backwards and forwards on the rope while the others sat around the Tarpit and watched him. Lucas liked to be admired. That was the thing that drove him. He went higher on the rope than anyone else. When it was almost at right angles to the tree trunk, he tucked his knees into his body and somersaulted through the sky. The water closed over him. I waited with his step-sister. The stillness and her unanswered question pressed down on me. At last Lucas surfaced and slammed his fist against the water. He looked up towards Tilda and me.

Then I heard Hamish shout, 'C'mon Captain Congo, shift

your arse and show us what you can do!'

I did not want to show anyone anything, but these were only boys. If they knew the things that I had done, they would be afraid of me. That is what I told myself. I turned to speak to Tilda but she had moved away. She was standing by the small grave that we had passed on our way to the waterhole. There was a stone angel at one end and someone had placed flowers on its head. Tilda's face was not smiling. It was as serious as the angel's. That girl is angry with you because you have not agreed to do what she wants. That is what I was thinking when I saw Tilda's stern face. I was surprised by what she said next and I wondered if I had been wrong about other things too. Perhaps the falling-down house would not matter to her.

'Whatever you decide, Manny,' she said, 'be careful of Lucas and his mates. I have to go now. My step-mother would kill me if she knew I was here.'

Tilda had gone by the time I got to the bottom of the hill and I was glad. I grabbed the rope and threw myself into the Tarpit. The water was cold and deep and dark like a never-ending well. Heads and shoulders blocked the light as I came closer to the surface. That is when I remembered Tilda's warning and that is when my lungs felt ready to explode. Pale hands reach down towards me. I knew who they belonged to. Lucas and O'Leary. They hauled me out, slapped my back and smiled at me.

23 MANNY

Twelve Thoughts

'Twelve Thoughts' was the name of the poem written inside the subway. I was like a detective following clues. I studied the handwriting on the wall. I compared it to the writing on the papers in my pocket and I was certain the same person had written them. Who is this person who wrote all three poems? That is the big question I asked myself when I was standing underneath the Bridgewater railway station. There was no doubt, I had discovered the identity of anon. I knew her name. It was Alice. That is who it was. The girl with long red hair. I saw her on the roof at night and again at the railway station, and although I was not close, I could see she had long hair. Hair right down to her waist. After she ran away from the waiting rooms, I found another poem. It was the one about a poet on a roof. When I saw her next, she was outside the scout hall. Her long hair was spread like a curtain on the green grass. Her poems were in my pocket. I had memorised the lines. Such hair, such poems, such things you do not forget. I would not forget that girl.

The subway walls closed me in. I forgot the smells and Tilda's warning and I read Alice's 'Twelve Thoughts'.

there are twelve months
twelve signs of the zodiac
twelve images of
twelve beautiful women buried
beneath cleopatra's needle and
twelve men have walked on earth's moon.
i wonder if any of them noticed
the stars
at oktober bend
and did i mention
that hercules was given twelve labours
for killing his family
or that a jury of twelve gave an old man
twelve years
for trying to avenge his?
but still i would rather be
twelve than not to be
at all.
anon

At first I tried to define twelve thoughts in Alice's poem. Then I stumbled on another truth. I smiled when I realised that the poem was simply a collection of facts about the number twelve.

If I had been braver I would have written a response to 'Twelve Thoughts'. I might have asked Alice Nightingale if the old man was real or imagined. I could have suggested another line about the men who walked on earth's moon, begging them to notice a small ruined country called Sierra Leone. I should have asked Alice if she was the girl in the poem and told her that if she was that I, too, would rather she was twelve than not to be at all.

But thoughts of Hercules weighed heavy on me. I had held the weapons that killed my family, but I had not stopped the men who did. Would I pay with twelve labours, and what would they be? How should I pay, and was running a labour?

Tilda Cassidy said everyone knew who I was, but how much did they know? And did Alice also know these things? Bull and kind Louisa James had offered me a new beginning in Bridgewater. I would be safe, they said, and so would my secrets. Was it safe to believe them? That is what I asked myself.

The house on stilts seemed empty when I arrived. I heard no sounds, saw no old lady on the verandah, no dog on the wooden steps, no Alice and no Joey. I found my way to the fishing hole in the river, where I had seen them last time. Footprints were stamped in the mud by the river. It was easy to follow them. Ten minutes later I found Alice and Joey swimming in a pool surrounded by large, grey boulders. Further on was the bridge that carried cars and trucks and bicycles in and out of Bridgewater. A crooked heart and childish letters had been carved into one of the beams that stretched its length, but I was too far away to read what they said.

24 ALICE

letting go

if i had known manny was there, i might not have felt so all
alone when i tried to let joey go. set us free.

i sank low
on the pebbled riverbed and watched
my words metamorphose into
pure and perfect bubbles
saw them rise and ride
the current
down-streaming,
imagined them floating
to the ocean
to canada and april,
didn't know
or care if i was
un-fifteen-like
i was
alice-like.

i stayed in my underwater world too long for anxious joey.
he hauled me back into his world of air and light, shouting
his little-boy name for me.

'birdie! birdie!'

i sat on the rocks, runny with river. tributaries trickled
from my hair and bear's tongue warmed my face. joey picked
our clothes off the reeds and tossed mine for me to catch.

'put them on,' he said, sharp-tongued, zippered his
cardboardy shorts, yanked his crumpled shirt over his damp
body.

i dragged my dress on, dry cloth awkward over wet skin.
watched the sun bleed pink and orange into the river. our
skins were dry when joey said, 'so...did you know crickets'
ears are on their knees?'

playful as a lamb he was now and i laughed out loud.
looked at his face to see if what he said was truth or lie.

'truth,' he said, magic at hearing words unspoken. 'and
they build burrows shaped like trumpets so's their mating
calls can be heard two football fields away.'

most days joey told me
at least one interesting fact
to make up for school cut short
because of what happened
one starry, starry night,
and the fear
that sometimes still
squeezed my lungs

froze my limbs and tongue and talk,
as though he thought
interesting facts would
somehow subtract all that
and the disgrace that followed
our family.

i thought about ears and knees and other parts of footballers while I waited for joey to speak again. but he said no more about the love life of crickets. he said other things instead.

'do you, i mean, i reckon... that girl called tilda's a good dancer, isn't she?' his words were as awkward as putting dry clothes on wet skin. as awkward as me. and i guessed that even my brother sometimes wondered how damaged i was. which parts were broken. which were not. and if i understood about different kinds of love. till then joey loved only me. loved me the way april should have.

but now there was tilda
and joey needing
clothes to cover
sex
that burned in him.
now we saw each other in new ways
were two not one
maybe more than kith and kin
maybe less kindred
and i knew

if ever i was going to grow
out of my twelveness
i had to get used to joey
loving someone else.

i turned my head away from him on my pillow of dandelions
and dock. closed my eyes to stop the trickles on my cheeks.
　　'sexy tilda,'
　　i said so he'd know
　　that i knew what it was like
　　to feel hot white fire
　　in all the places
　　that made me
　　girl.

the laughter i laughed for my brother sounded ugly. false.
but sometimes even brothers do not hear emptiness and
pain. they are listening to their own joy. joey's arms went
around me. grateful. glad he had to say no more. i stayed
there with my heavied heart until the sun was gone, not
knowing what would happen now. how to be. wondering
if brother love was big enough, or if this was the beginning
of forsaking. then we walked home slow as winter treacle
along the river track, under the bridge of never-forsaking.
together and apart. our new separateness mysterious and
strange.

25 MANNY

Keeping Tilda Safe

Only two days had gone by since Tilda Cassidy came with me to the Tarpit. It was Friday. I did not think I would see her again until the following Wednesday. I was not ready to see her. But there she was, under the trees outside St Simeon's. I tried to make myself invisible in the middle of a group of boys passing through the gate and did not look at Tilda. But I am tall and black and she darted to my side, small and neat in her navy blue dress and white socks.

'Hi, Manny,' she said. She looked up at me, waiting. All she wanted was to know where Joey Nightingale lived. But I could not speak, not even those few words. Especially those few words. Not now and maybe not ever.

I had seen Alice and her brother in the river. Their bodies were not the bodies of children. But they played like children in the water. I was once like Alice and Joey. Before the soldiers came I did not know what it was to feel dirty or ashamed. I wished I could feel that way again. I did not want anyone else to find the house where Alice and her brother lived. I did not want anyone else to see what I had seen, to spoil what was unspoiled. I would not betray the Nightingales.

There are people who can make you say things you do not want to. I have known men like these. 'Tell us where your mother is, boy, and your sister will be safe.' That is what they said. But they were liars. For all I knew Tilda might betray me, or if not Tilda, Hamish O'Leary or Lucas Stewart.

I remembered Tilda's small hand in mine. I remembered how she said she hated her step-brother's friends, and I remembered her stony face when she warned me about them. I saw them now, leaning on the school fence not far ahead. They were watching us. Perhaps they were waiting for Tilda. Perhaps they were not. But I would not tell the coach's daughter what she wanted to know. It would be best, I decided, if I had no more to do with Tilda Cassidy. I did what I did to keep her safe and to keep the Nightingales safe. I kept walking and I lied.

'I have not had time yet,' I said.

'See you after dancing, next week then?' she said. But I did not answer. I stepped off the footpath and crossed the street. I knew without turning that she had not left, that she was standing with her small, neat feet together on the curb watching me go. They all were. It was hard not to run.

between the cracks

like kites cut loose
in the gunmetal sky,
we danced
higher, faster
more daring than safe
more brave than afraid
the ballerina, my brother, the stranger
and me.

sometimes i didn't know this new joey. yesterday as familiar
as my own skin. today a riddle to be solved.

one night i heard him arguing with gram. when it was
quiet, i slipped into her room. crawled in beside her. she
stroked my hair. tried to work her buggered breathing
apparatus. i tried not to listen. thought about how easy
air slipped in and out of me. i looked at the moon while i
quietly filled up and emptied out. thought about the men
who once walked there.

'maybe joey could get you one of those oxygen tanks,'
i said.

'where'd he get one of them?'

'he'll know.'

'i aint goin' near no damn hospital.'

'joey won't let that happen.'

'you never know what he might do, that boy,' she said.
'one minute he's sweet-talkin' me, callin' me his glory girl.
next thing he's pinching me pension money.'

'he only does it when the fly money runs out. we have to
eat, gram. he's trying to look after us.'

i didn't want her getting mad with joey. getting mad
was one step nearer to not loving. i wished i could explain
about joey trying to get free. peeling off from me. pushing
off from her. getting himself separate. tell her it might take
a while for him to get used to being properly fourteen.

'i'm done wastin' my breath on that boy,' she said. 'he's
got his grandpa in him.'

she said it like there was something wrong with that.
wrong with old charlie, who'd maybe done more for me
than the rest of my family put together. done time.

the morning after the argument, joey said, 'want to come to
ballet with me tomorrow?'

he didn't tell me what mrs cassidy said. that it might be
best if he didn't bring me anymore. that my last seizure had
disrupted the class. i said yes. i didn't want to dance but

i was still hopeful a feather would fall, my wish would be granted, the tall dark boy would be there.

'we'll bring bear,' joey said, boyish and cheeky and charming. 'she can wait under the steps. old ma cassidy won't even know she's there.' old ma. that's what he called her. i knew then he didn't like her. didn't know why. didn't know she'd warned her perfect step-daughter to keep away from boys like him. didn't know that tilda had told joey.

i met his cool green gaze
saw the straight line of his jaw
the shadow on his lip
the spread of his shoulders
and wondered
for how long
he'd been
this way –
hard and beautiful.

joey lifted the rice canister down from the mantelpiece and took a banknote from gram's pension money. we'd used all faulkner's fly money. i felt sick in the stomach because of what gram said the night before about joey stealing.

'i think gram's getting funny,' i said. 'funny in the head.'

'why? what's she been saying?' he answered, quick and sharp, and i decided not to say anything about the money.

'nothing.'

'i s'pose she's been whingeing about me.'

'her breathing's getting worse.'

'and what am i s'posed to do about that?'

'there's oxygen tanks…'

'hell, alice, grow up! you can't just walk into the chemist and ask for a tank of oxygen.'

i felt as twelve as i ever had.

'what are we going to do?' i said and joey answered, 'shit, i haven't got answers for everything.'

my brother had always known the answers before. had always been sure and strong. but now he needed to be fourteen and gram needed more than we could give her and it was hard being just me when i'd been part of us for so long. i closed my eyes and saw our separation scars, felt the pain of them zig-zagging like sharks' teeth between our hearts.

joey wagged school. caught a bus to kalinda and spent the money on black tights and a singlet with narrow straps. for him, not me. i wondered how mrs cassidy would feel when he peeled off his baggy shorts and her perfect step-daughter first saw joey in his dancing skin.

no songs or stories or interesting facts spilled out of joey on the way to the scout hall. but he crackled with strange electric energy. pedalled hard and fast with my dancing slippers tied to the handlebars and me on the parcel rack, legs out wide. wide like they used to be when i was a little girl. when the only thing you had to be careful of was not getting your feet caught in the spokes. joey's straw curls, bunched with string and feathers and beads, bounced between his bare brown shoulder blades. bear ran beside us and for a little while our separate hearts seemed one again.

'we're too early for ma cassidy,' joey said.

propped his bicycle in
the square black shade
behind the hall
showed bear her place
leaned his head
over the gully trap
turned the tap and
opened his mouth
the water went
in him and
over him and
when he straightened himself his
sunburnt hair was scattered
with diamonds.

he was dazzling and for a heartbeat i wished he could be mine forever. then tilda came.

when she saw joey her eyes grew wide and her lips came apart. but mrs cassidy was at her side. eyes like lizard slits. mouth a red gash between nose and chin. joey went to meet them. stood tall and straight.

'i've come to join beginners' class,' he said. his voice

deep and cool as the river. he took more money out of his pants and tilda took the skin-warmed notes from his hand. mrs cassidy said nothing. but i saw joey's sweet, cruel smile. watched perfect tilda trying not to laugh.

when the seven beginners lined up at the barre, it was tilda's job to teach them. joey was the only one taller than her. the only one with hair on his face. the only boy. when he dropped his shorts i went outside and crawled underneath the porch. i lay in the dust beside bear who was transformed by the slats and the sun into an odd striped beast.

i wondered if i could learn to like tilda even though she was so perfect. or if she could like me. could mrs cassidy ever learn to like joey? perhaps she'd once had a brother like mine.

a boy so much part of her
that there was no you or i, only we.
had they left their clothes on a bank somewhere and
dived into the river like wild things?
had he cared enough
to explain the whereabouts of crickets' ears, or
steal books and paper and pens for her? was he
the sort of brother
who used hammers and chisels as tools
of tenderness to carve private promises
in public places?

was mrs cassidy's mouth a thin straight line because she had lost a boy like mine? or was it because she was afraid of never being loved by perfect tilda? did she worry that tilda might love a boy whose sister had crazy wiring? maybe hattie fox had filled her ears with gossip about my papa, charles patrick garfield nightingale. or the things that happen to girls who don't keep their knees together. i never had to think about these things when joey loved me best.

bear rumbled. i opened my eyes. she rumbled again. a shadow fell on my face. and the stranger was there. tall and dark with french-knotted hair, looking between the cracks. looking at me.

27 MANNY

The Sound of Anon

Alice climbed out from under the porch, holding the dog by its collar. It was the closest I had ever been to her. There were cobwebs and leaves in her hair. I stood still and let the dog smell me. When it was satisfied, Alice beckoned me come and I followed her. We sat in the sand near a swing made from a truck tyre. Our feet were bare. Our shoes hung around our necks on laces and ribbons. The sun was hot on our heads and her hair was like fire.

'I am Manny James,' I said, and she nodded and smoothed the white sand with the palm of her hand. She wrote slowly and carefully with a stick:

i am not a bird
i am not a mermaid
i am alice.

I reached into my pocket and pulled out the poems. I did not expect to hear what came from Alice when she saw them. It was the strangest sound, thick as porridge and shapeless, like the speech of someone who had never heard a human voice. That is what it was like. Or something far worse. She looked away and I hoped that my surprise had not shown on my face. I held the poems in front of her.

'Did you write these?' I said.

Her eyes flicked over them and she reached for the writing stick.

'Tell me,' I said.

I wanted her to speak. I did not care what she sounded like. I wanted to see inside her mouth. I needed to know she had a tongue. That is when I made a very big mistake. I put my hand on her arm. It was not a smart thing to do. I heard a warning rattle in the dog's throat and then it bared its teeth. Alice touched its flank and it sank quietly to the ground beside her. Their eyes never left me.

'I'm sorry,' I said. 'I did not mean to scare you. I know that you wrote these poems but I just wanted you to tell me.'

Alice frowned as though she was confused.

'I want to hear you say the words,' I said in case she mis-understood. The seconds ticked slowly by and lines of her poem ran through my head.

my soul is filled
with songbirds
but when i open myself to
set them free

they shit
on my lips

I remembered the nightingales and the silence they left behind them when war came. I remembered the brave silence of my sister, the sounds of soldier's lies, my mother's screams and my baby brother's cries. I saw my sister's open mouth and the pool of blood as she lay at the soldier's feet, forever silenced.

Now this girl was in front of me. Alice, with my fingers still wrapped around her arm. The tendons in her throat pulled tight, I saw her lips, her teeth and tongue and I knew what was happening. Alice Nightingale was opening the cage to set her birds free. Trusting me to understand, that is what she was doing.

'I am Anon,' she said and still she watched me. Her eyes were green like new rice. She was waiting for me to look away, expecting me to. But I did not. I could not look away from this girl. Then she smiled at me.

28 ALICE

things i wrote

on the pages of alice's book of flying it is written:

once upon a time, a boy with no yesterdays asked a girl with no tomorrows for something no one else wanted. the sun was high and bright and the almonds had burst their mouse-coloured vests when the boy came.

there was nothing at all to remind the girl of long ago when she was twelve years old. this boy did not come like a thief in the night to steal what was not his to take. he stood before her but did not touch the hidden parts of her; the little hills of cream beneath the folds of her clothes, the things that made her girl. all that his hands held, on that shining day, were her words.

then he told her what he wanted, not knowing it was the hardest thing of all to give. he wanted the sound of her.

29 ALICE

things i did not

i did not write what happened next. did not spoil the pages of my book of flying with the dark things joey said to me and manny james when he and perfect tilda came running and running with bear's early warning rumbling in their heads. alarm drumming too loud in joey's ears to hear my heart's calm, blinding him to bear relaxing at my feet, misunderstanding manny's hand around my arm, not knowing he held me soft as a velvet cuff.

i am glad now that i did not write about my brother, fierce as he was, that day. trying to allow me to be fifteen, but not being able to break the habit of protection. remembering the night we never spoke of. and me so slow to make words to tell him it was all right to leave me and manny alone. angry he wouldn't give me time to find out if i could be fifteen. afraid i'd never discover if a boy like manny james could want to know a girl like me.

when joey was at last out of words, manny introduced himself and said, 'i am sorry if i have offended you. i am still learning the customs of your country. i only wanted to speak to alice.'

he spoke clear and plain and when he'd finished, reached out his hand to joey. it seemed to take until forever till my brother unclenched his fists. three times their palms met. three soft smacks. i counted each one in my head then let my breath loose.

before their hands cooled, i heard other voices. voices that reminded me of the smell and sound of a football team up close. i remembered the panic, the falling, and worst of all, the memory of manny being there, watching my body jerking out of control on the grass outside the hall.

suddenly afraid i couldn't explain my crazy electrics, even to a boy who didn't turn away when i spoke. i called bear and ran away as fast as i could.

30 ALICE

old charlie's table

when i was in danger of coming unstuck, it sometimes helped to think about old charlie's table. i read somewhere that when a cyclone or an earthquake or some other act of god is about to happen, it's safer to get underneath something. i didn't know if you could call a person an act of god. gram said god made us. joey said bullshit, only sex makes people. i did not know or care who made manny. he came with no warning. stepped stealthy as a cat on the powdery dust of the long dry summer. bear and me, curled as peach leaves on the ground under the scout hall steps, had no chance to run, to hide. home is where i ran when the bombers came. home to papa's table. that is where i went and where i held myself in my arms. i didn't know what else to do.

my grandfather built his table square so no one would ever be too far from the others around it. it was his gift for his children, he said. but no child of his would ever claim it. the timber was sawn from a river red gum that washed loose from its moorings one spring, when the sky let go and the river rose up and seeped through the timbers of our living room floor.

the floodwater found its way to the sea. the mud crusted over and old charlie called in a favour from hattie fox's brother, who trucked logs for a living. he towed old charlie's tree to the sawmill. years went by till the wood was good and dry. then they milled two slabs for the tabletop, squared four posts for its legs. dave williams rounded their corners off with his lathe. old charlie carved lion's paws on one end of the legs. dovetailed the joints, fastened them together with dowels instead of screws. when his table was built, my papa carved his name and the names of his family on its surface: charles patrick garfield nightingale, gloria nightingale, lola nightingale and sunny james nightingale, and the dates of their birth. he rubbed it smooth as glass with a wad of steel wool and polished it with beeswax and turpentine.

my name and joey's were added when we were born. and when his face was all gullied with sorrows, old charlie carved the dates of the deaths of his children. lola's five months to the day after she was born. my daddy, sunny-jim's, when he was thirty-two.

gram said the table looked like a tombstone. took to slicing bread on it; sawing away hard and fast as though the bread was a month old. pretended not to notice when the knife's serrated blade chewed into the wood underneath.

she screwed the mincer onto the table's edge, grit her teeth and turned the wing-nut till the metal plate bit savagely into the timber.

when she wasn't using it, gram covered the table with an old curtain. by the time i came home from hospital, the curtain was gone. replaced by lino glued to the table top, fastened tight with tiny tin-tacks that old charlie used to mend the soles of his boots. the lino was brown, patterned with red and orange leaves. left over toilet lino. joey begged gram not to do it. said it would break old charlie's heart. i was lying on the divan they'd dragged into the kitchen. my words all taken away.

'and what about *my* heart?' gram said. 'i don't need no words scratched on a table to remind me my babies are lying in the ground.'

that's what she did, our gram, covered things over.
didn't talk about them
pretended they weren't there
linoleumed the table
painted over
the pencilled-in
markings that measured
my father's height
on the door jamb.

but outside
under the rainwater tank

        two pairs of handprints pressed
        into the concrete slab
        old charlie's doing
        minding kids
        mixing concrete
        he pressed baby lola's
        pink and perfect hands
        then sunny's into
        the soupy, half-set concrete,
        precious reminders like
        fossils from another time,
        a time when
        the nightingales sang.

old charlie's table was too big for three, gram said. she had
joey push it hard up against the wall. as if the lino was not
enough, she began to cover it with other things. piles of old
newspapers, skeins of knitting wool, empty cereal packets,
odd socks and canned food. she took her meals on her lap
in the rocking chair by the stove. joey and me sat on the
verandah steps when the weather was fine, or at the kitchen
bench by the window where we could see the glint of the
river between the tepees of climbing beans and corn rows.

while i was under the table i tried to remember if i ever ate a
meal in someone else's home. ever sat at a table that wasn't
old charlie's. and i wondered if manny's people had built

a table. did his daddy make it big enough for family and friends? and small enough, so people never felt too far away from each other? did manny watch patient hands smooth and carve and polish? did his little boy fingers trace letters on its surface, learn how they looked, how they sounded, what they meant? did he feel safe between the lion's paws planted firm on the floor of his grandfather's house?

as i lay wondering, a thought came unexpected. an idea, sweet and sudden as a blackbird's song. i crawled out from between the lion's feet. went to the kitchen window. rows of empty jars were lined up on the sink. through the window i saw gram in the garden picking milky-green tomatoes, last of the season. gram picked them slowly, tumbled them gently, by the apron-full, into polystyrene boxes. later i would help her make pickles. should have gone to help her harvest, but didn't. wanted to start on my idea before anyone could stop me.

quiet as a thief i worked. took everything off the table. levered tacks loose, opened the door to the stove and stuck the blade of the carving knife into the firebox. summer and winter gram kept the fire burning. without it we had no hot water, nothing to cook on. i waited till the knife glowed red hot, then slid it under the awful toilet lino. the glue stank and melted. again and again i heated the knife. bit by bit i uncovered the top of old charlie's table. piece by piece i stuffed chunks of lino in the stove and watched them burn through the window in the firebox door.

while i worked, i planned what would happen when i'd finished. after i'd polished the table with beeswax, i'd run my fingers around the curves of my father's name. feel his days. we would sit together around my grandfather's gift: manny and me, joey and gram. elbows touching. no one would be too far away. ever again. we'd share our table and our food. and fill the silence with names: old charlie, sunny-jim and aunty lola. i don't know why i thought manny might be able to help me do all that.

gram saw the smoke from the garden, stinking black clouds of it.

'what do you think you're doing?' she hollered from the wash-house door.

'fixing papa's table,' i hollered back.

she shuffled into the kitchen and leaned on the door, catching her breath. looked at the table. shook her head and said nothing and i did not care. it was too late. the lino was gone and i was fixing things.

31 MANNY

A Fisherman's Table

In poor villages, like mine, there were no books. The only stories that we knew were the ones our fathers told us. These stories were the ones that our grandfathers had told our fathers when they were boys. Their stories were not written on paper. They were memories; that is what they were. When the war came, it took everything that was good from my country. The only things that I brought with me to the house of Bull and kind Louisa James were the stories that my father told me and memories of my own.

Sometimes Louisa James invited me to tell my stories.

'Tell me about your country, Manny.'

That is what she would say. For a long time I could not. I would ask myself, what would a fine lady who lives in a house of glass make of my stories? What would she think of the house where my family lived? What would she think of the sleeping mats and the fire-pit, the windows with no glass and the table that my father made?

My father made his table from pieces of driftwood that

washed onto our beach after a storm. The wind and waves had worn it as smooth as sharkskin. The salt and sun had bleached it silver-grey and pieces of sea glass had lodged themselves in cracks and bolt holes. The sea glass looked like tiny rock pools. That is what it looked like. The timber came from a shipwreck, my father said. I remember how hard he worked dragging it from the beach to our village. He built his table outside under the branches of the cotton tree and that is where it stayed. My father's table was very big. It was long enough for twenty people and wide enough for many bowls of food to share. That is how big it was.

We lived in a small coastal village, not so far from Freetown, the capital city of my country. My father was a fisherman. My mother worked for a rice farmer. She planted and picked and threshed and cooked, then served it with my father's catch to me and my brother and sister. When war came to our part of the country, there were others who sat with us at the table. They did not have to be asked. Cousins and neighbours, strangers and travellers – they all came. Some were searching for their families or safe passage to another country and they needed a place to sleep. Other people came because they were hungry. Some of these people brought mangoes or pineapples to share. Others had nothing to give. They came with empty hands and tales of burnt villages and stolen children. My mother fed them all. Some nights, after they had gone, my father would sit alone at his table and weep. My grandmother said that her son sat with the ghosts of the lost and cried for the living. All grandmothers have sad stories to tell.

Bull and Louisa James shared their table with me and would have shared it with others, too.

'Why don't you ask some friends home, Manny? Invite them for dinner.' These are the kinds of things they said to me. And when I told them that I did not have any friends yet, Louisa James said, 'What about the boys you play football with?'

'I do not think those boys are my friends,' I said. That was a fact. That was what I thought and that was what I told Louisa James.

'Maybe if you ask them around, you'll get to know them better.'

But I was not listening. I was thinking about a table for twenty. I was thinking of how long it took to build and how quickly it burnt when the soldiers set fire to it.

'Well, just think about it. When you're ready.' The voice of Louisa James was gentle and her eyes were the colour of the sea, and I hoped that some day I could tell her about my father's table.

32 ALICE

my grandmother's chest

joey stopped asking me whether i wanted to go dancing. i guess it seemed like i was getting harder than ever to understand. not the sound of me, but the things i did or didn't do. running away from manny, the boy i clearly wanted to be near. the only boy who'd ever asked to hear my voice. joey wasn't the only one who was confused.

i didn't miss ballet lessons but i missed joey urging me to come. i missed wrapping my arms around him, feeling his body move as he pedalled, and the laughter that followed us. i wondered if i would ever hold someone like joey again. someone who knew everything about me and loved me just the same. or rather, if someone like that would hold me.

i never saw joey in tights again after that first day. but he still left at the same time on wednesdays. still said he was going to ballet. but he never said anything about tilda. or manny. it felt like another silence was growing. i wanted to stop it by telling him my idea about the table.

'you could bring tilda.' i'd say it like inviting people to

eat with us was something we did all the time. 'we could have real spaghetti. the kind that doesn't come in cans. and you could make your famous bolognese sauce,' i'd tell him, although he'd never made it for anyone but me. there'd be billy buttons on the table and unchipped plates. i never thought about my own silence or what would happen if i did speak when tilda's perfect elbows were almost touching mine. thoughts of seizures didn't trouble me. i'd be home, safe; bear beside, lion's paws beneath.

'maybe gram'll make apple pie,' i'd say. blanking out the shortness of her breath, the slowness of her walking.

one wednesday, when it was time for joey to leave, i watched from the verandah.

'what's up?' he said throwing his leg over the bike. for a second i wanted to climb on behind him. sit on the parcel rack like nothing had changed. wondered if fifteen was hard for everyone, or just for people like me.

'you can come with me if you want,' he said. i shook my head and went inside. filled a flask with tea and made cheese sandwiches.

'c'mon, gram,' i said. 'come with me while i bait the shrimp nets.'

'long way down there.'

'no it's not. c'mon, i made tea and sandwiches.'

gram was slow. it took us much longer than i thought. we sat on the rocks in the sun, gram and bear and me. when gram's breathing steadied, she cut chunks of soap from a yellow laundry bar. i wrapped them in gum leaves, put them in the nets and dropped them into the river. when they were all done i poured the tea and we shared the sandwiches. the food and drink loosened gram's tongue.

'good job you done of the table,' she said. 'shame ol' charlie's not here to see it.'

'it'll still be there when he comes home,' i said. i'd given up asking when we could go and see him again.

'that's if he gets outta there alive.'

'he'll come home.' i said. inside i wasn't so sure. 'maybe we should use it,' i said.

gram blew small brown ripples across her tea. sucked in a few slow sips. i didn't expect her to answer.

'it's too big for three. 'minds me of all the others who should be there.'

'we could ask other people. to fill the gaps.'

'no one would come,' she said.

'why not?'

'because we're not like them. we're different.'

'you mean they're not like me, crazy in the head. is that why you won't let me ask anyone – because i talk funny? because of the fits?'

'of course not. it's nothing to do with that.'

'what then?'

'people talk about us.'

'tell me one thing they say that matters. one thing.'

gram didn't answer.

'so, if i ask someone and they say they'll come, that's okay?'

gram looked at me, kind of desperate, then she said, 'there's my chest.'

of all the excuses she could have made: my weirdness, her drinking, old charlie, the falling down house – she'd chosen her chest. her chest! if she'd said, 'because i'm sick, because my lungs are ruined' or 'because i've got emphysema,' i would have replied, 'we'll do all the work. joey will cook, i'll clean.' but gram said, 'there's my chest,' and i surprised myself. as smart-mouthed as any teenaged girl, i said, 'what about your chest? is it too small, too big, too saggy?'

laughter bubbled out. i couldn't help it. i laughed and laughed and it felt good. even better when gram joined in. we lay on our backs on the lumpy rocks and wobbled and hollered. sweet, salty tears streamed from our eyes, down our cheeks, and vanished behind the lobes of our ears. when we were done, when we both got our breathing under control, i said, 'what the hell, gram! i met a boy and i'm going to ask him to come and sit at old charlie's table and he's not going to take any notice of your chest!'

i never thought to mention colour.

33 ALICE

a question of colour

when bear and gram and me got back to the house i made iced tea with lavender, lemons and honey. i told gram it was a potion for her chest. and we smiled at one another. but the laughter was gone. i went upstairs and put on a blue dress. i never wore blue. hated the dress. one of the country women's ladies gave it to gram for me. it was a hand-me-down of her daughter's.

'tell her blue goes well with red hair, gloria,' the woman said, as though i wasn't there, as though she couldn't see me standing beside gram. 'those bright pinks and reds she wears aren't really suitable for a redhead.' then she looked at me. 'i see she has green eyes,' she said, 'but i shouldn't worry about that. no one else will notice.'

the day i got that dress, i took old charlie's shaving mirror to my bedroom and held the blue dress under my chin. it looked like i was pretending to be someone else. should i have known the rules of colour? were they something else i had forgotten? i stuffed the dress in a drawer and took

out my book of flying. then i climbed on the roof and took
a bird's eye view of the world before i wrote down my
questions on colour.

who can tell me if
the tail of a peacock
is incorrect or
who messed with grapefruit?
ruby flesh?
orange rind?
and anyway
whose idea was it
to make grass
green and sky
blue?
furthermore is evil
always black?
or does it come in blood
red?
on the other hand if black is
only wicked
shouldn't someone change the colour
of midnight or
is that what
stars are for?
and just one final thing, is that girl
with crazy wiring the only one

    to think
    autumn is beautiful and that
    the rainbow is a work
    of genius?

i had always wanted to use the word furthermore.

34 ALICE

in a field of significant weeds

i remembered that poem and the reason i'd written it as bear and me walked towards charlotte's pass, the long dry grass catching at the hem of the hated blue dress. i'd left gram in the living room, snoring invisible clouds of lavender-scented breath. at teddy's grave i put a piece of garden china and a feather in the angel's broken fingers. then i tucked the hand-me-down dress into my underpants and crawled up the cutting. bear made a dog-nest in the grass and i, in my dress of invisibility, fitted into the couch like the last blue piece of a jigsaw puzzle.

joey and me had talked about how the couch got to where it was. sitting near the top of the cutting, hidden from the road by the safety barrier. he said it might have fallen off the back of a truck. maybe the driver didn't know. or maybe he did and couldn't be bothered dragging it back to the top. or maybe someone just dumped it there, joey said. it had been there for as long as i could remember. the midnight blue faded to the colour of forget-me-knots. the soft pile, the difference between ordinary cloth and velvet, wore off. sunlight and rain bleached the wooden armrest white as horn. but still you could see it wasn't an ordinary couch. at one end was a curved, cushioned back. it held you like an arm around your shoulder. the other end had no back at all. it was a couch properly made for putting your feet up. an elegant couch.

in spring, thistles covered the walls of the cutting with purple heads the size of tea cups. woolly grey leaves folded over like rabbit's ears. the thistle had a proper name, recorded in the book of significant weeds. it is onopordum. the elegant couch also has a proper name. it is chaise longue. if heaven exists and if there are couches there, i think they will be chaise longues.

    sometimes when planes fly by
    i imagine the pilot and
    his passengers among them
    a truck driver jetting
    his way
    to the forty-ninth
    parallel or to london where
    the weather is mostly
    grey
    his drowsy holiday
    eyes turning towards
    a window catching

a fleeting glance of his
long lost
couch caught like
a scrap of sky in
an amethyst sea
of significant weeds.

one long-ago morning, when mist made the rabbit-ear leaves almost invisible, i flew over the amethyst field. over the forget-me-not couch. over teddy's angel. a helicopter rotor chop-chop-chopped urgently at the clotted-cream clouds. and i inside, heard nothing, saw nothing. i was on my way to a hospital in the city. no one in bridgewater knew how to help a girl like me.

i came home by train in summer. stopping all stations. the steeps of charlotte's pass rising up outside our window. sun-dried thistles strewn like the rib cages of dead animals at the feet of the elegant couch.

but almost four years have passed since then. on this day, i lay on the couch watching what was present and waiting for what was to come. i wished for manny to come. to sit beside me at old charlie's table. lie next to me on the couch, our hearts held close by its one curved arm, our legs twined together down its blue narrows.

but wanting manny to sit with his elbows touching mine would not make it happen overnight. i remembered how long the god of flying things had made me wait till manny came that first time, and tried not to think of how i ran away from him.

i might have mentioned before, how gram had a saying or a song for every occasion. one of her favourites went something like this:

'god sometimes likes you to take the initiative.'

joey said that was hedging your bets. he said gram invented it because she wouldn't admit there was no one up there to answer her prayers.

that day, in the hand-me-down dress that clashed with my eyes, i gave gram the benefit of the doubt and god three weeks. the furniture and i were ready. i was shouting on the inside. a fist raised to the sky.

35 ALICE

anthem

a flock of cockatoos rose like rags in a dust devil. i heard the bridgewater bombers before i saw them running towards the tarpit. i felt invisible on the forget-me-not couch. its faded arm was around my blue shoulders. the footballers far away, ran circuits up around the barbecue and down again carrying bricks. one in each hand. in small towns like bridgewater, people make do. manny ran with them. even from my distant perch on the couch i could tell it was him. i wished he ran alone. boys in bunches sometimes dare. sometimes call down ravens like sorcerers call down spirits. maybe manny was more like other boys than i'd thought. i imagined a wall made of forty-four bricks. wondered if it would be big enough to keep me safe.

there is courage and there is caution, gram says. when you are twelve until forever it's hard to know which is which. so i waited while the bombers trained, scared to leave, scared to stay. not sure if i was brave or stupid coming here in the first place, hoping to speak to manny. gram said we should learn from our mistakes. i was twelve years old when i made my biggest mistake. it happened the night i went shrimping, when i stayed on the hill to watch the stars above oktober bend instead of following papa and joey to the river.

at last the bombers threw their bricks in a heap and the coach left. i willed the others to go with him. wished manny would look up. but the sun was low and i couldn't wait. i had to be home before dark. when i stood up someone shouted. one of the footballers stabbed his finger in my direction. others turned, shouted some things i couldn't hear and some i could.

'moron! slut!' they yelled and laughed.

i wanted bracken tunnels to swallow me up in their darkness. wanted to disappear myself down a wombat hole. but the bridgewater bombers stood between me and those secret places that only me and joey knew. i dragged myself the short distance to the top of the pass. found my feet and ran along the horizon, close to the burning crack between heaven and earth, near to the light. bear ran with me, her breath warm and loud on my heels.

fear swelled inside me. fear i'd be followed. the railway station lights winked on. the train pulled in. bear and me rounded the waiting-room door. people were everywhere. i slid down the wall. hunched in a corner. alone in the crowd. bear and me. the grass-stained skirt of my dress had ripped away from the bodice. i wiped my eyes and nose with it. pulled it down over my knees. joey wasn't there to keep them together. bear barked. the birds were coming. sometimes she heard their flapping wings before i did. i opened my mouth. a raven's voice scraped at my throat,

'fetch joey!' it said, 'fetch!' and bear ran.

light stroked the lids
of my eyes and i
wondered if i
had fallen
into the crack between
heaven and earth that place
where the sun is
swallowed up between
the violet lips
of dusk.

i know a song about cracks. i heard it when i was in the rehab hospital. most people there were old, but the lady in the bed next to me was about my mother's age. she was like me...her electrics were shot. they said she'd had a stroke. with me it was words. i knew them but found it hard to say them. with her it was arms and legs and smiles. the messages from her brain didn't get through. her smiles were stuck on the inside, and one side of her worked and the other side didn't. with the fingers that worked she pressed a button. played the same songs over and over.

the song about cracks was my favourite. it's called anthem. i wasn't sure what the words meant. but the song is a poem and poems mean whatever you want them to. in rehab i told myself that the message was about how things aren't always perfect but they can still be beautiful. even broken things.

anthem was playing in my head. someone was stroking my arm. the frosted ticket window was shut. the waiting room was empty. no one was waiting for trains to come or go. but manny was waiting. he was waiting for me. i wanted to ask him if he knew the song about cracks.

heroes and villains

joey came, fetched by bear. frightened, i imagine, to see bear's loneness at our door. he confronted us at the orchard gate. glance as sharp as glass, took in my face, torn blue dress, filthy knees.

'where have you been? what have you done?' his hasty words accused.

weariness swayed me. i could find no voice to explain the tear-tracks, the ripping and the filth. looked to manny. dusk all around him like a hero's cloak. venus, the evening star, bright as a medal over his shoulder. boys did not rescue girls like me. till then old charlie and joey had been my only heroes.

manny explained about my falling down in the rail-way waiting room. he did not speak of the couch on the cutting. i was grateful that he kept the secret of my stupidity. wondered if he had guessed that i had done it for a glimpse of him, for a chance to speak to him again. now we were in league, manny and me and wise bear, who sat in a comfortable heap at my feet. i trusted joey would see reason; villains did not take their victims home. they prowled like wild dogs, taking what they wanted, leaving the rest lying under the stars.

into the house manny came, with joey holding the door. my grandmother sat in her chair by the stove. closed her hand around manny's. while she looked him up and down and in his eyes, i scrubbed my knees in the wash-house. ripped off my torn clothes. dressed again in watermelon pink and tied up my tangled hair. when i came back manny was on the verandah, talking on a mobile phone. telling someone called louisa james that he'd be late. the door to the stove was open. the coals were red as hell. gram was toasting thick slabs of bread with a wire-handled fork and joey was frying green tomatoes and poaching eggs. i set the table. no cloth, just feathers in a jar and paper placemats; sheets of music from my book of flying. bird songs in case there were silences to be filled. wanted manny to see papa's engravings, wanted him to know that we nightingales were once like other people.

there were fewer silences than there might have been during that first shared meal. hope prised open the tiny doors of my caged heart. twice now manny had seen me fitting. twice he had not turned his back. he had listened to fragments of my stumbling speech and begged me to speak again. his wanting to listen made no difference to my speech. it was no clearer, quicker or more fluent. my words did not sound like birdsong or poetry. but manny watched me and waited while i spoke. asked me when he didn't understand. laughed with us when we laughed at my mumblings and his misunderstandings. that night we had everything we needed – food for our hunger and conversation for our souls.

when our meal was ended and when manny was swallowed up by the night, joey helped gram upstairs to her bed. i lay myself across my grandfather's table, held up by the lion's paws. put my cheek to the timber. smelt the beeswax. my tears became rivers and streams shaped by the names of my family. i cried because manny had come, had given me hope. because of him i tried to forgive those absent for leaving. those present for having so little faith in me.

37 MANNY

Shame

Louisa James wanted to know where I had been. I did not tell her that I saw Alice on the couch or how worried I had been about what might happen if the others saw her. There are some words that you do not say in front of a lady like Louisa James. I could not repeat what I heard those boys call Alice. Most of all I was ashamed that I had not tried to stop them. I could not tell her that.

'I have to catch up with the coach,' that is what I told those other boys before I sped off down the river track. I guessed that Alice would have to go through the railway waiting room, and that if I ran fast enough I would meet her before she got home. I wanted to know if she was all right.

I cannot forget how Alice looked when I found her. Her bright hair was ragged, her dress was torn and her face was white as rice. But I did not speak of these things to Louisa James.

'Her arms and legs jerked and I could only see the white part of her eyes. It was an awful thing to see, Louisa James. There were many people in that waiting room. Some of them stared, but most of them pretended they did not see. Not one of them offered to help. That is a fact.'

'Perhaps they were afraid, Manny. Some people are, you know. You could have phoned me. I mightn't work now, but once a nurse, always a nurse. You can count on me, Manny. Any time.'

'I know that, but there was no time.'

'How did you know what to do?'

'I am not sure if I did. I remembered what I saw her brother do and copied him. Then I waited with her until it was over.'

'You've seen it happen before, then? You know these people?'

'I did not know them that first time. It happened at football training. The girl used to go to ballet lessons. I was waiting to go in to the hall when she... when it happened.'

'Well, I'm pleased you stopped to help, Manny. Proud of you. Her parents must have been very grateful when you took her home.'

'I... they were not there. Only her brother and the old lady.'

'Her grandmother?'

'Yes, her grandmother.'

'So they live near the station?'

Louisa James wanted to know more than I was ready to tell her.

'Does it matter where they live?' I said, and straight away I knew I sounded rude.

'Of course not. I thought you knew me better than that, Manny.'

I loaded the dishwasher. Then I opened my homework but it was very hard to concentrate. I had disappointed myself, twice over. I was a weak person. I had promised myself I would protect Alice, but I had not tried to stop those boys calling her names. And now I had spoken rudely to Louisa James. Kind Louisa James who would not hurt anyone. That is one thing I knew for sure. But I wanted to keep Alice to myself for a while longer.

Cocoa repairs many problems. This is one of the beliefs of Louisa James. Sharing cocoa with another person repairs even more problems. That is another one of her beliefs. While I was trying to do my homework, Louisa James made two mugs of cocoa. Then she switched on the television and patted the red leather couch beside her. There are many things to learn in a new land. Some of those things have no words at all. I do not think a word exists that describes the meaning of two mugs of cocoa, the television speaking softly in the background and the hand of Louisa James patting the red couch beside her. This was a new language. I learnt it with my eyes and with my heart. All of these things together meant, *Come, sit beside me, I have forgiven you. Now, forgive yourself.*

Forgiving myself always was the hardest thing. I watched the news with Louisa James. I saw the pictures but I did not hear the words. I was thinking about that old couch at Charlotte's Pass and I was wishing I had been sitting on it with Alice, so I could have protected her. I did not know how. Perhaps we would have been invisible to everyone else. When I was with her I felt as though we were the only two people in Bridgewater. Then a thought came to me. Why had Alice been sitting on the sofa? This was something I had not thought about before. The news finished before I could reach a conclusion. Louisa James pointed the remote control at the television and commanded it to be quiet.

'Your friends are always welcome here, Manny,' she said.

'Yes, I know,' I answered.

'Your new friends too, the girl... what did you say her name was?'

If Louisa James had not been a nurse, she would have made an excellent detective. That is because she was good at asking questions. A good memory is also an important thing for a detective to have. Louisa James could remember almost all the names of the Bridgewater babies she had helped to deliver. But that is something I did not know when we were sitting on the red couch repairing ourselves with cocoa and Louisa was asking me the names of my friends.

'Alice,' I answered, and it felt good to say her name

aloud. 'Her name is Alice and her brother is called Joey. But they are not really my friends, just people I have met.'

'Well if ever...'

'I know, Louisa James,' I said. 'Thank you.'

Louisa James is a very smart person. Instead of always asking questions she sometimes told me things instead. She made them into stories, like my father did, so that I would remember them.

'We didn't always live in this house, you know,' she told me when our cocoa was almost gone. 'Michael's parents divorced when he was thirteen years old. He was the oldest of seven, the youngest was still in nappies. His mother worked two jobs and Michael took care of everything else. I think that's where he got the name Bull. He just went at everything head-on. He was only eighteen when he started his earthmoving business. All he had was a crowbar, a pick and shovel, and a hired trailer. His motto, "Bull James Moves Mountains", was like a prediction of the man he'd become. There's no shame in being poor, Manny,' said Louisa James, 'none at all.'

She always left the most important thing until the end of her story. That was the thing she wanted me to remember. Sometimes it took a long time for me to understand what her stories were really about. I understood that this story was not just about Bull. Louisa James was telling me that I did not have to feel bad because my family was poor. That is what I thought, and I wondered if I should tell her that

I did not know my family was poor until I came to the house of windows.

But if I had known, then, about Louisa James's very good memory of the names of the babies, I might have guessed that she was also talking about Alice and Joey.

troubled

'that boy is troubled,' gram said on the morning after manny had sat at old charlie's table.

'i thought you liked him,' i said.

'it's got nothing to do with whether i like him or not. we just don't need no more trouble in this house.'

her breath rasped and she huddled close to the stove. i was angry but i bit my tongue. if i wanted manny to come again, i'd have to be careful not to upset my grandmother. besides, she had ways of knowing that other people didn't have.

i remembered the look i'd seen in manny's eyes that first time. the day i lay on the small grassy hill near the bicycle rack outside the scout hall, when he gave joey his handkerchief to wipe my face. i thought he was afraid. frightened of me the way other people were when i had seizures. last night proved he wasn't.

i hoped gram wasn't right. i should have warned manny not to let glorious nightingale hold his hand. should have told him to do his looking anywhere but at her. but i was not properly back from where i'd been. my thoughts were foggy. unwisely i left the room, and manny with his hand held in my grandmother's, while i went to tear off my rags and tatters and clean my knees.

while i was worrying about what gram said, joey came into the kitchen wrapped in a towel. he spread honey on his toast and licked the knife and said, 'he was probably just nervous', and i loved him all over again. not for daring to disagree with gram but for defending manny. i stepped outside and into my boots and ran, full of glee and anger, down to the woodheap where i could not hear what my grandmother said.

troubled. what is troubled? i asked myself as i picked up the axe. i swung it above my shoulder and drove its blade down. down into the grey box and into the yellow box. and down again into the stringy bark.

troubled is the faulty functioning of a mechanism of the mind or body. i'd memorised this explanation from the dictionary. alliteration can work like a remembering tool for people with damaged electrics. and even for people whose electrics work perfectly fine most of the time. faulty functioning, mechanism of the mind – simple.

in my own words: when the equipment that makes your body or mind work is damaged, people often describe you as being troubled. it was plain to see that manny's body worked just fine, so what kind of 'troubled' had gram seen in his eyes? what other sort was there, except mine? if i had read further in the dictionary, i would have found troubled described this way: *to be disturbed or worried.*

perhaps then i would have turned to page 231, where i would have discovered that to be disturbed is to be: *emotionally or mentally unstable or abnormal.*

a dictionary is like a map made of words. who knows where these might have led me? maybe to gram, who trusted no one and tried to even out life's ups and downs with cheap wine.

some of my body machinery worked perfectly. i smelt sap and felt rhythm in my shoulders. the axe head buried itself in the sweet, dry timber. the thud of metal and the splintering of wood sailed up my arms in rivers of quick-running blood. anger oozed with sweat from my pores. i pushed a barrow-load uphill and stored it under the house. wheeled another onto the verandah. stacked it outside the wash-house door. i was good and tired and emptied out when i carried the last armful inside.

gram had dozed off by the fire. she slept less and less often in her bed. preferred to sit by the fire, sipping endless mugs of scalding water poured from the swan's-neck spout of the kettle. i reminded myself to talk to joey about moving her bed into the kitchen before autumn was ended.

i shoved the wood deep into the belly of the stove. kissed the top of my grandmother's head and wondered if love and hate were twins.

while gram slept, i took the dictionary down. turned to the page where troubled was also described as: *to be disturbed, worried or upset by something unpleasant.* i wondered if it was normal for a fifteen-year-old girl to ask a boy if some unpleasant thing was disturbing, worrying or upsetting him.

when joey left for school, i walked with him. his small gesture of siding with manny had made a difference. together we strolled through the orchard. our feet shuffled the scarlet leaves and the orange. the early air iced the backs of our throats. we were almost to the fence when joey said, 'when are you going to bring manny home again?'

my heart slammed against the cage of my bones.

joey looked at my bright cheeks and laughed and said, 'i might ask tilda, too!'

his smile was gorgeous, generous and rare. he was gone through the hole in the fence before i could speak.

i walked proud that may morning. proud i'd brought manny home, maybe not with words, but he *had* come – and it was for me he came. i didn't let myself think he might have done the same for any fallen-down person. joey, with all his words and charm and learning, had brought no one home. he spent more and more time away from our place. sometimes, when i looked at his lettering on the bridge, i felt forsaken. joey was with tilda, i was almost sure. but the way he looked at me that morning, and the things he said, made me feel as though i truly was fifteen. truly his older sister. and our separateness did not hurt quite so much.

all the way home, i planned what we would do, me and manny. all the things i would show him, the places i would take him, the secrets we would share. i imagined gram falling under manny's spell the way i had. she'd say, 'tell that boy of yours to get himself down here. i'll make beef stew with suet dumplings tonight.'

i never considered my grandmother shutting manny out. out of our conversations. out of her heart. i never thought we might have to wait until she was asleep by the fire. that we would creep upstairs like thieves in the night and sit on the roof under the stars. or lie in the boat under the house with the other hidden things: the book of kells, the cadbury's roses tin and the double-barrelled shotgun. i never wanted to hide. hiding is what people do when they are afraid or ashamed. i was neither.

39 ALICE

forgotten thing

the air cooled. leaves crisped and curled. i chopped barrow-loads of firewood. frustration greased my joints. made the axe swing smoother. blistered my palms. but i could not decide how to invite manny to our home again. i blamed the bridgewater bombers. after what happened at charlotte's pass, i never wanted to be near them again. would not go to the scout hall or sit on the lost couch in the field of significant weeds. this was caution, i told myself. i was no coward. letting manny hear me speak was proof of that.

even joey made me mad. twice in the past few weeks he'd brought tilda home. they'd sat at papa's table. made manny's empty place stand out. gram talked to tilda while she was there and kept her mouth shut when she was gone. said nothing to joey about tilda bringing trouble.

'what about family business?' i said to joey after tilda left the second time. 'i thought we were supposed to keep quiet about family.'

'you brought manny,' he pointed out.

'i didn't ask. he just came. brought me home because you weren't there!' anger hissed out of me.

'i can't be with you all the time, alice. anyway, i know you wanted him here.'

his voice turned to caramel. 'why don't you ask him?' he urged me again.

'too many people at dancing,' i answered. my voice had lost its fire and i couldn't mention charlotte's pass.

'write to him. you're always writing. go on, write and i'll give it to him.'

'what about family business?'

'manny's only interested in you, and tilda won't say anything.' my cheeks grew warm again and my tongue felt too big for my mouth. i wished manny and me could be like joey and tilda – nothing seemed to worry them, stopped them doing what they wanted to.

'how do you know she won't talk?' i said.

joey upped his shoulders and turned away.

'i just know.'

'but what if she does tell.'

'tells what? tells who?'

'maybe her father…you said he's a policeman. what if she tells him i don't go to school? what about gram? how old she is. her breathing.'

i didn't want to think about what would happen next. or speak of it. but winter was on its way. we'd made up the bed beside the fire for gram to sleep on. her breathing seemed worse every day. and joey and me were nowhere near eighteen. my brother's face looked grey and hard as teddy's angel.

'tilda won't say anything. she doesn't tell her family she's with me. she says she's with a girlfriend.'

'why?'

'because we're not like the cassidys and their friends! shit, alice, haven't you noticed?'

joey's words flung into the air then fell into place, rearranged like scrabble tiles. i saw a list in my head:

daddy's dead
mother's missing
sister's crazy
grandma's sick
grandpa's jailed.

so what? i wanted to scream at the top of my broken voice, *that's who we are and if other people are like the bombers and mrs cassidy and swindling jack faulkner, i'm glad we're not like them!*

instead i looked at joey's face before he turned his back on me. and i sorrowed for us all. but mostly for my brother who was not twelve until forever, who was older, much older, than fourteen. who'd gone to get a good education and learnt it would be easier if we were like everyone else.

at seven-thirty that evening joey still wasn't home. i thought he might never come back. mist blanketed our bend of the river. gram's breathing was bad. i tried not to let her catch me looking at the clock. pretended i was going out for more firewood when i was straining my eyes, looking for a pinprick of light moving towards me along the river track. a beam from my brother's bike.

'he'll be home soon,' i said, praying i was right, when gram asked me where joey was. 'and when he comes, i'll ask him to ride to the post office and get hattie fox to phone the doctor.'

'no you won't,' she wheezed. 'they'll cart me off me to hospital and that'll be the end of me.'

and the end of us? i wondered.

'here, put some of this on me,' gram said.

she handed me a small blue jar and held up her singlet while i rubbed eucalyptus ointment on her back.

i stoked the fire and got into bed with her, my chest against her back, arms around her shoulders. bear lay on our feet. sometimes i wished i had the sort of grandmother who went out like other women did. to country women's meetings, or the supermarket, or to have a cup of coffee with friends. sometimes i could hardly stand to be in the same room as gram, listening to her trying to suck oxygen into her stuffed-up lungs. but i couldn't picture the house on stilts without her.

after a while her breathing grew quieter and i thought

she'd gone to sleep. i eased away, ready to step out, go to my own bed. bed was the warmest place in the house on nights like that. then gram spoke; her voice was drowsy, dreamlike. a voice from the past. like the one she'd used to tell me stories when i was little.

'there's things i never talked about before, birdie,' she said. she used joey's pet name for me. she never did that. i was frightened. maybe gram was dying. right now. damn joey. where was he?

'i never knew when was the proper time or if i was the right one to tell you. but i haven't got forever,' gram went on.

'don't talk now gram,' i said. 'go to sleep.'

'it's gotta be said,' gram gripped my arm. 'i've been wrong about a lot of things. maybe i was wrong not sending you to school. you don't talk so good, but that's not your fault. doesn't mean you're not smart,' she said, and i relaxed a little, pleased with gram's praise. what she said wasn't much, but it was better than nothing.

gram began to cough then, as though something was caught in her throat. perhaps it was the cold, star-spangled air or the words she'd kept from me for so long. i pulled the blanket over our heads, pressed myself closer, willed her lungs to keep working. lay in the tartan dark wishing joey would come.

when at last gram's breathing steadied, i slid off the bed, fed the fire and tucked the blanket in. gram rolled over on her back and reached for my hand. i could not leave. i waited, hungry for more words of praise, hopeful gram would tell me other things. tell me how my mother loved me. how she held me, words she used to comfort me, songs she sang, looks she gave me, gifts that only a mother can give her child. i was wrong to wait.

'those boys done you wrong, alice,' gram said. 'hurt you bad and took what wasn't theirs to take. but they never took all of you. you're more than what people can see and feel and hear.'

i should have stepped away. should have snatched my hand from hers and covered my ears before her words opened my tight-locked door of forgetting.

'you're more than what's between your legs. a lot more, girl.'

truth, suffocating as a river of tar, flowed from my grand-mother's mouth. i knew what had happened to me in words. the reality had been locked away. when gram spoke of it, i lived the nightmare again.

jelly-legs stumbled me to the sink for a dish-cloth. i tried to stuff it, grey and sopping into the pit that was my grandmother's deep and horrible mouth. she clawed at my hands and ravens dashed their wicked beaks against the panes and flew down the chimney. soot devils. bear would not be quieted or consoled. she leapt at their battering wings and i swung the broom. around and around i whirled, scarecrowing the demon birds, scrubbing my grandmother's words off the walls. walls that eddied and fell and me with them. the ravens pick-picked at my herringbone stitches until muck oozed between my thighs and i crawled between the lion's paws and cradled my crazied head in my hands.

joey's arms were around me when i came back. the tartan blanket gathered us in the bed by the fire. gram in her chair, rock-rocking. her shut eyes, blind as teddy's angel, turned towards the red glow of the stove. no sodden rag in her mouth. just slow breath. rasping in, rasping out. joey stroked my mad red hair. smooth were his strokes, smooth as butter, and wet were the shadowed planes and angles of his face. deep in the valley of his nightingale throat he crooned a lullaby. never forsaking. never forsaking his troubled sister. never. my let-me-go brother. my let-me-go watch-me-fall brother. watch me fall he did that night. then cradled me. golden boy. brother.

'why did she?' said i to him. 'why did she think i would want to remember?'

40 ALICE

still alice, still

what french-knotted boy would come now to my door?
would sit at my grandfather's table, warm elbows nudging?
who would lay his back in the everlasting arm and twine his
legs with mine on the narrows of the heavenly couch? what
boy now would smooth my skirt, would fetch me back from
where i'd gone with soft talk and stroked arms? what boy
would walk me to my door if he knew the reasons for my
strangeness? would carry my poems against his velvet skin
like love letters from my soul to his?

i stepped out. out of my self. out of my window onto the
balcony, into the night. looked down to the place where no
boy would ever stand and wait. for me. bear beside me. i
climbed where she could not follow. onto the roof i went.
up the steep of it where it jutted black against the cheese-
wheel moon. joey followed. never forsaking. quiet he stayed
beside me. i kept my silence beneath the stars. asked for
nothing and was given nothing in return. no roof-top poems

came to me. i was noah in his ark. floating in a sea of dark. no land in sight. no island of refuge. no tree, no branch, nor twig; no place for wrens to perch to sing their songs. time was no more. when i turned, joey breathed a column of pure white smoke and his hand reached out to me. frost had cast a crystal cloak on the rippled tin. we slipped and slid. on bellies, thighs and palms we came down, but i felt nothing. joey led me to my room and i lay down and he beside me with bear at our feet. nearest and dearest both. and gram downstairs as unpicked as me by what she had done and undone. hemmed in by love i was. unforsaken, although i did not feel it then.

mornings later, while all the world still slept, i stole the canvas bag down from its peg behind the wash-house door. i checked for the tobacco tin full of hooks. bright, sharp, hooks. made sure my grandfather's fine-pointed scissors, his heavy-pointed scissors, his clippers and dubbing needle were all inside the soft leather pouch. i put the strap of the bag over my head, crossed my heart with it. then i walked towards oktober bend. river songs in my head. hooks in the bag on my hip. constant companion left behind closed doors.

the sky was bruised, dirty yellow and grey. i stopped at the elephant rocks where my grandmother and i had laughed about her chest. i lay down, spread me thin and close to the ancient grey beast to feel if an imprint of our laughter was pressed into its skin. a curling, rippling fossil of sound, captured forever for anyone who cared to stop and listen. perhaps seekers of that elusive thing called joy, recorded in days past by scribes and scholars, lovers and poets. but the river drowned its secrets and the stone remained silent. i cushioned my head on my grandfather's bag. thoughts came to me of the book and the two glued pages. i remembered fish with rainbows on their skins, bloody red gills and gaping mouths. i saw the pure white coat of the man holding them and his face; his eyes closed as though he couldn't stand to look at what he'd done. i saw the coat of the surgeon who sewed me up with his needle and his thread, his mouth was covered so i could not read his lips, but the spell of twelveness was in his eyes. then i remembered my grandmother's face after she spoke the words that called down ravens. her eyes, red-lidded, tight shut.

i raised my cheek from its canvas pillow and unscrewed the lid of the tobacco tin. opened its mouth full of bright sharp hooks. careful, my fingers unfastened the leather bag and laid bare the scissors and the needle. i laid them side by side; the hooks, the scissors and the needle. forgotten were the silks, the linen threads, silver tinsel, peacock plumes, the furs and fleeces. forgotten were the muddler minnow, the priest, the demon, the damsel fly nymph and the micky finn. before me were instruments to cut and slash, to probe like doctors' tools. cold and steely.

in the morning mist, under the cold new sky, i took off my clothes. peeled off my watermelon jumper, with pips and rind and soft pink flesh all knitted by lumpy grandmother hands. red pants next. do-not-go-with-hair-like-that pants. underpants last. made to keep privates private. off i took them. the river whispered siren songs and i stepped quickly into its icy embrace. greedy, it lapped at my thighs, circled my waist, fingered my breasts and raised them up. weedy fingers touched me. gentled me. cleansed me. took me under. held me down with the silent stones and the darkling fishes. and i, at that moment wishing, wishing to be unborn.

the last of my breath was a string of pearls. my face an underwater moon. there was no angel in the dirty morning. no jesus walker on the water, no brother waiting on the bank to haul me in. no dog to remind me with tongue and tail what it is like to be loved, dirty or clean, whole or broken. no everlasting arms to carry me home. no anthem. only me. alice.

and in me a seed of hope. enough to draw me up towards the crack. towards the light.

i dragged my clothes on. took my pen and inks from old charlie's bag. set them all upon the elephant rocks beside the silver hooks and the scissors. then i took out my book of flying and turned its pages until i found one that was empty. on it wrote.

i am alice
still i am
alice
no less
no more
just different
alice

i left the book unshut, beneath the pale sky for all to see. or no one. or for me alone. alice. alice with the seed of want. wintery sun fell on my watermelon shoulders and on my moss-green words. while they dried, i took old charlie's fine-pointed scissors, his dubbing needle, a reel of silk and a peacock quill and prepared to tie a lure.

41 MANNY

Running to Alice

I had promised to help Tilda Cassidy find Joey and I had not. But they found each other without my help. I saw them often at the scout hall. I had been afraid for nothing. It was clear that Joey trusted Tilda. But no matter how I looked for Alice, I could not find her. And I could not speak to Joey about Alice, not while Tilda was with him.

Could I go to the house? Was that permitted? I was fed and clothed. I had shelter. I was in need of nothing. What were the customs of need and want in this country? Could I visit uninvited? Could a person knock and ask for his heart's desire? Was that an acceptable reason to knock? These were the things I wondered while I searched for signs of Alice.

When I ran at night, I stopped on the bridge to watch the windows of the house where Alice lived. I hoped that she would step through her window and climb onto the roof the way she did that first night. I wanted to see her again, sailing through the stars, that is what I wanted. And in the early mornings I looked for her. I thought that I might see her disappearing through the hole in the fence behind the railway waiting rooms with that very large dog beside her.

My thoughts were more often of Alice and less often of the places and people of my childhood. When I ran, I told myself that I was running towards the future. Towards Alice. That is where I wanted to be.

It was morning when I found her. She came out of the river, so pale that I thought I might have dreamt her. I was afraid to turn away in case she vanished. I saw her twist her hair into a rope and squeeze the water out, onto the smooth grey rocks. Then she dressed herself in bright clothes and I knew then that she was real and not a dream. That is when I thought that I might be able to stop running for ever.

42 ALICE

a decent thing to be

an elephant is
a creature large
enough on which to rest
an open book
a girl
a boy
materials for making
fishing lures and fire
made of sticks and stalks.

down to the river came manny james. through the wilder-
ness where we nightingales hid ourselves away from the
rest of the world, he came. he lit a fire for me. quiet he
did it, without asking or telling. without any saying at all
he gathered twigs as thin as wren's legs, grass stalks and
leaf litter. like a bower bird, he built a tiny tepee of his
gatherings on the rocks where gram and me had laughed.

i was surprised to learn that manny knew how to build a fire. one night joey and me had walked past the big houses on the other side of town. joey showed me where tilda lived, and manny. he told me there were no fires inside houses like theirs. people had only to press a switch to make warmth come up through the floor. manny took a cigarette lighter from his pocket. warmth came into my body even before his fire was built on the rock. his being there was better than the sun.

when the fire was well alight, we went in search of bigger sticks to feed it. under the bridge of never-forsaking we went. manny's eyes lifted up to joey's lettering and i saw questions in them that he did not speak. we dragged little logs back to the fire. my legs perfectly happy in their red pants. even in winter, watermelon warms the heart.

joey and bear were waiting when we got back. bear wrapped herself around my legs. inhaled my happiness and licked my hands. joey kept his surprise inside. i never saw anyone else do it so well.

'just checking the shrimp nets,' he said, like it was normal to see me with manny at the river in the early morning dragging little logs to our fire, me first, him following. my brother walked to the river's edge and hauled in a net. it was too cold to expect a good catch.

'there's enough for two,' he said. 'i've gotta get home to gram. i'll leave bear here.' i was too busy feeling the miracle of manny's nearness to remind joey that bear answered only to me.

we threaded shrimps on sticks. cooked them over the coals till their shells turned orange. peeled them and ate the sweet white tail-meat. licked our fingers and wiped them on our clothes. then manny turned his eyes towards the unshut pages of my book of flying, curved like scrolls in the warmth of the fire. he saw my moss-green words and after i had nodded my yes to him, he read what i had written. many times he read it and the morning was quiet. fishes sipped gently at the damp grey air and water spilt like silk over ancient rocks. manny looked at me and asked,

'what made you different, alice?'

the sound of his question was like longing on his tongue.

on my grandmother's dressing table was a photograph in a small oval frame. the frame was silver as a fish's skin with a border like barley sugar twists. two small feet at the bottom kept it from toppling over. it was the sort of frame a person would hold dear, not one to leave behind if they were journeying to the forty-ninth parallel never to return. in the background of the photograph was a water tank on its side filled with firewood. in front of it was a child wearing blue denim overalls and a striped tee-shirt. the little girl had bare feet. her right hand was on the handle of a small, wicker doll's pram with wheels the size of biscuits. she looked away. away from the pram. away from the person

who held the camera. perhaps her eyes followed someone
who was leaving. perhaps even then she knew her mother
would not stay.

    i have looked many times
    at the photograph in
    the barley-sugar frame at
    the side of the turned-away face
    the small right hand
    on the handle of the wicker pram
    at the denim overalls
    the striped tee-shirt
    and the bare brown feet
    and i have tried
    to remember what it felt like
    to be me
    before
    i was different.

it isn't easy to tell someone why you are different when you
are not sure exactly how different you are. a girl cursed with
twelveness has no measure of herself because she cannot
remember being three. doesn't know what anyone else
feels like when they are twelve or fifteen.

    i looked at manny across the flames. i did not want to
speak of what was past and done. but i had other things to
tell. my frayed and fractured voice joined other sounds of
morning. the small, near songs of frogs and bellbirds. more

distant screams: cattle in the slaughter yards, the foundry whistle. the sounds of all of us mixed and stirred. the ordinary orchestra of life.

'the words are in me. but harder to say than write,' i told manny james.

'you are much better at writing than me,' he said.

'i'm slow…need time to get the words out.'

he nodded. answered, 'i do not mind waiting. i will learn to listen like your brother does.'

so far, so good, but i wasn't sure how much more i wanted to tell him.

'you do not go to school?'

'i used to. before my head injury. joey brings me books now. teaches me new things. looks after me.'

'yes, i know. i saw him at the scout hall. that is when i saw him first.'

'sometimes i don't fall down for a long time.'

'the falling down, is that because of the accident?'

'no accident.'

'i thought that you said…'

i shook my head.

'they meant it.'

'i do not understand. what happened?'

i could not meet manny's eyes. he had seen me come out of the water. that i did not mind. my body made me something like other girls, but i had things to tell that would let him see into the darkest places of me. i fixed my eyes on the flames. made a list in my head.

'i was waiting for
joey and old charlie we
came every night i
sat on the hill with
the lamp and
counted stars while they
checked shrimp nets
no one ever
came before just this
one time.'

bear pressed herself close to me, put her chin on my lap. and i went on. spewed the words like dark ravens into the flames, crimson, marigold and rose. each one took more effort than the last.

'two of them came crept
like robbers put
their hands over
my mouth
to keep my screams
inside while they did
what they did

to me and afterwards
the tall one afraid
i would tell
heaved a rock
overhead then
smashed it down and
down and
down while the other
one tried to stop him they
argued shouted wrestled and
the lamp fell
glass shattered and set
the grass alight
flames for danger for
warning for old charlie and joey
to come
running.'

quiet then. all my dark sayings burnt to ash and bone and blown away. me emptied, aching, raw as if i had swallowed swords. manny's arms gathered me, and in their strange new circle i thought a dazzling thing. the one who most needed to know that being alice was a good and decent thing to be was not manny james. it was me.

'i am alice,' i whispered, and my words fell new-made against manny's shoulder.

'still i am
alice
no less
no more
just different
alice
still.'

my voice had not changed but my words were a song.

43 ALICE

river sonnet

manny stayed until late afternoon. when he said he must leave, we went with him. bear and me. took him along our secret route to the railway station. i led, manny followed and bear came last, our feet quiet on the earth. only crickets in their trumpety holes could have heard us. my magic hands unlocked hidden tunnels through the towering grass. ours was a quiet kingdom of plants and earth and air. too soon we came to where the fence was a wall of weedy creepers. i peeled back the corner. manny took my hand. stepped through. would have taken me with him. but i shook my head. guilty for leaving gram for so long. anxious joey would be angry.

i watched manny pick his way across the shunting yards. haul himself up on the platform, disappear through a doorway marked 'travellers' rest'. saw him again, smaller, in kennedy street. two boys approached him. their faces far away, unknowable. but it seemed clear they knew manny. they jogged beside him towards the scout hall. bombers, i thought. over there is manny's world. a world of friends, football, school and big houses. i pushed the wire back into position and ran home.

'where've you been?' asked gram. sour as green apples. 'a woman could be dead, for all you care.'

'the river,' i said, jamming logs into the fire. wishing i was jamming them down her throat. wishing i'd gone with manny. wishing for someone to share my happiness. i made a pot of tea. spoon-fed gram with buttery sops in thin chicken soup.

'where's joey?' i asked, guessing he was somewhere with tilda. mad he hadn't stayed with gram.

gram shrugged.

'you all right?' she said. better now, with some food inside her.

i nodded. felt strong. *still alice*, i told myself. *no less, no more, just different alice.* different from what i was yesterday. different because manny had searched for and found me.

after i'd fed gram, i emptied the bucket she peed in, filled a basin with warm soapy water, washed her face, hands and feet, rubbed ointment onto her chest and back, and helped her into a clean singlet and nightgown. i brushed her silvery hair and braided it, and when i tucked her into her fireside bed she took my face in her hands and my heart by surprise.

'you're a good girl, alice.' she said. and even after what she'd done to me, what she'd said last time, her unexpected words left me wanting to climb in beside her. under the tartan rug with nearest. with kin. tell her all i knew. ask her what i didn't. say i love you.

instead i went outside. stood beside the rainwater tank under a tree hung with oranges. tiny planets between glossy leaves and sprigs of blossom. i picked one, peeled it and separated it into segments. twelve small sticky smiles. i took them inside and ate them at old charlie's table with my back towards my grandmother.

later, i spread the tools of my trade on old charlie's table. the inks glowed like jewels. the empty paper awaiting the touch of a nib. i wet my pen and marked the page. i wrote in claret and finished with gold. a recipe i wrote, for a lure yet unmade.

name:	river sonnet
type:	dry streamer
hook:	#3
thread:	pearsall's gossamer silk
body:	purple silk ribbed with silver tinsel
hackle:	sacred ibis – dyed kingfisher blue
wing:	peacock

faulkner would never set eyes on this lure. but i made a

note at the bottom of my page. imagined it as it would appear in one of his advertisements.

note: *this unique lure was conceived by bridgewater fly-maker, alice nightingale, as her response to a pact made with the god of flying things. and although its design is practical, the river sonnet is not intended for use as a fisherman's lure, but rather as a collector's piece. a fine example of the craft of fly tying.*

i smiled to myself when i read it. then i heard a soft thud as joey's boots fell by the door. heard his muffled footsteps cross the floor towards gram. i lay down my pen, twisted caps onto ink bottles while my recipe was drying. when joey saw me he came and sat at the table. read what I'd written.

'have i seen this one?' he said.

i shook my head. 'i haven't made it yet.'

'i like the label. sounds like something faulkner would write. it's good. really good. professional.'

'thanks.'

'let me know when you've got enough ready for faulkner.'

'this one's not for him,' i said.

'oh?'

'it's for manny.'

gram snorted in her sleep. turned over in bed. joey looked across at her.

'about the other night,' he said, 'gram probably thought she was doing the right thing. you know, when she said –'

'it's okay,' i said. my grandmother's words, short-circuiting electricals and the things they made me do were not something i wanted to go over.

'd'you think she's going to die soon?' i whispered. 'is that why she said it?'

'i dunno, alice,'

'but you're not eighteen yet.'

'don't worry about it. want some soup?'

he filled two bowls from the saucepan on the stove.

'i went down to the river again, before i left. you looked like you were okay…you and manny,' joey said. i didn't answer. too busy thinking about me and manny. his making fire for me. me leaning against his shoulder. telling him things i'd never told anyone before.

'tilda says he's a good bloke,' joey said, and his words took my air away.

'you talk about me and manny? to other people?' i said.

'only to tilda and only once. i asked her what she knew about manny, that's all. he's in the same year as her brother… they play football…'

'but you said my name and manny's together?'

'i don't know, i might have. geez alice, you're my sister, can't i mention you?'

it's okay. 'mention' is different to 'talk about', alice nightingale, i reminded myself. *that is what other people do.*

178

joey finished his soup. wiped the bowl with bread.

'i'm going to bed now,' he said. but he didn't. he watched as i began to draw a cover for my label. i blocked in the 'n' for nightingale. the pencil strokes on the page calmed me.

'i don't want anyone to hurt you. that's all,' joey said.

'i'm almost sixteen. i can look after myself.'

'sixteen,' he said, 'so you are!' he messed my hair and i let it be. this time i did not hear the sound of his feet on the stairs. or my grandmother's breathing.

    i sketched
    flowers and feathers and
    fish that i modelled on the beautiful
    book of kells
    amongst the other
    creatures, damselflies and liliums
    in the place
    where joey's face had always been i drew
    a dark boy with troubled
    eyes french
    knots on
    his head and flames
    in his hands.

it was cold when bear and me at last climbed the stairs. i pushed my bed across to the wall where the kitchen chimney came up through my bedroom floor and out through the ceiling. pulled the blankets over my head. lay on my side, back to the chimney bricks, bear at my feet. heat seeped from the bricks into our bodies. i was asleep in moments. but not before i wondered if manny james had asked anyone what they knew. about me.

44 ALICE

letting manny in

manny came often in the school holidays. sometimes we
worked in the paradise garden with joey, pruning fruit trees
and grapevines. lopping willows by the river. binding the
cuttings into sheaves to dry under the house. saving them
till the winter solstice of the following year.

before papa went away, we celebrated the solstice every
year with a bonfire. when my skull was split open like a
pademelon, not all memories of before were lost.

fragments
became tangled in the rosy spikes of bottlebrush
woven into wattle-and-daub nests of river swallows
and drowned in the sticky throats of correas
even our sandy river flats sparkled
as much with memories as with micah

and i, despite my fishbone stitches and crazy wiring, still
remember the excitement leading up to those smoky, black

velvet nights. in the weeks before, joey and me spent days loading anything that would burn on our pram-wheel and pallet billy cart. nights we spent under the house. a bare bulb burnt like a caught sun in a wire cage while we two fashioned twiggy arms and legs. papa fastened them with a bag needle and string to a straw-stuffed potato sack. i can't remember gram ever being there. it was always papa. papa with no religion, no faith except in me and joey, who tried to teach us what little he knew about traditions in sweden, the place where our mother was born. where snow fell like mae petals at christmas time.

in the land of our mother's people the longest night was celebrated in december, with bonfires and candles. it was called saint lucia's day, after a girl who was good and kind.

'what's a saint, papa? is it like an angel? does it have wings?'

old charlie wasn't sure. 'a halo, maybe. dunno about wings,' he said.

papa said that the longest night at oktober bend fell in june. said we could build a bonfire then. we small nightingales liked the idea of angels and saints, wings and fire. even joey did. so began a new tradition on the longest night of the year. the paradise garden was decked with hurricane lamps. an orchard angel floated above the bonfire. joey and me sat on the rocks. papa stuffed a kero-soaked rag under the sticks. stood back and tossed a match. we watched in awe as our higgledy-piggledy tower of sticks exploded into flames. orange, yellow and scarlet licked at the angel's potato-sack skirt and brown-paper wings.

i remember the first year we burnt the angel, how old charlie looked behind us into the dark. i looked too, to see what it was that caught his attention. lamps winked in the apple boughs. beyond them and above, our kitchen window hung in the sky like a painting. a picture of gram, standing at the sink watching the fire. watching us burn the angel. papa turned back to us.

'i might have got this part wrong, kids,' he said. 'i'm not sure if the saint's supposed to burn.' but happiness was ours then. we worshipped life. danced on the elephant's back and drew pictures across the face of dark with red-tipped sticks.

we never celebrated the solstice after papa went away. gram said she was scared a stray spark might set fire to our old house. joey and me knew different. it was because she couldn't think of anything worth celebrating.

sometimes, still, i see her staring out from inside the kitchen; i think about the bonfire and the angel. about the window hanging in the dark. gram in the kitchen. i wonder what she was thinking then. wonder what she was thinking when she watched manny work with me and joey. hauling prunings under the house on the billy cart. mixing whitewash. painting the trunks of the fruit trees to stop the bark splitting. was it the trouble she'd seen in manny's eyes that made her watch him? or was it because she liked him? was it both? another person to love, another to lose. was that what she thought? was that the reason she never invited him in?

but i did
i let him in
through a crack
in my heart i let him come
the day he found me lying
on the little hill of green
my broken mind whirling
giddily
into my waking
and sleeping
he came and now
into my home and up
the stairs i let him
in.

on the floor of my bedroom i spread my lures. manny, on his knees beside me. wanting to know why i had made them and of what. wanting to know everything about them. about me.

'papa taught me when i was ten. small fingers tie tiny knots. i didn't forget.'

'does he still make them?'

'he didn't take his tools,' i said. not saying where papa was gone. not yet. that was his story. i thought it might be a betrayal to tell manny.

'could you send them to him?'

'he doesn't need them. i make all the flies now.'

i showed manny my collection of
hair and hide
fleece and fur and feathers found
on fences in
fields and forests.

he looked at my dye pots. i told him the ingredients i used to make them. when he saw my labels, he sat back on his heels and shook his head.

'you made these? you really made them?'

i nodded and wondered if manny would say words like the ones faulkner did. instead he said, 'these are gold!'

'joey bought the gold out of the fly money,' i said, mistaking his meaning.

'no, alice, i do not mean the ink. in this country, if something is very excellent, it is the custom to call it gold. your labels are gold!'

we laughed at my mistake, like gram and i had laughed on the elephant rocks. then i asked manny if he knew what 'comeuppance' meant and he didn't. so i told him about jack faulkner and how joey found out he was underpaying me. i explained how then i'd made labels for the lures and sold them to faulkner for fifteen dollars apiece.

'joey said that was faulkner's comeuppance for cheating me on the lures,' i said.

'so comeuppance is when a person gets the punishment they deserve? is that what it means?'

'something like that,' i said.

'do you think faulkner deserved to be punished?'

'he thinks i have no brains because of how i talk. i wanted to see his face when he saw my labels. that was best, not the money.'

my voice was tired from the many words i had already said. i wanted to go out on the roof. wanted to show manny my special place. i fetched my book of pages, undid the latch on the window and pushed it open.

'come,' i said to manny.

'will you be okay?' he asked.

'i am safe here. never fall. not once,' i said. we stepped out onto the balcony. i showed manny the best way to climb up to the ridge. showed him how to grip the iron. where to put his hands.

'like this,' i said. 'with hands and knees. if you slip, you'll slide, not fall. the chimney will stop you.'

we perched like birds on
the nightingale nest

our knees scabbed
with roof moss
the house hemmed in
by the rain-fattened river and
the railway
we watched the ebb and flow of
day and night
over our frail winter
garden of sticks
and stalks scratching
the swollen stomach
of the low sky
saw the far and away
spires and steeples and ordered streets
the many-windowed
homes and all
the other glories of
men glowing small
as worms in the mouth
of infinity.

a freight train broke the spell. trundled past the silos. hooted
a husky warning at the foundry boom gates. i opened my
book to put words to the things i'd seen and smelled, heard
and felt. a loose page from an exercise book fell out. manny
slammed his hand on it. stopped it slipping off the roof's
edge into space. he turned it over.

'may i read the writing on this paper, alice nightingale? would you mind?' he asked hesitating to give it back to me.

it was a story. one of my first tries when i was relearning to write. some of it was true, some imagined, because no one was willing or able to tell me all that happened. heat swarmed through me. i mumbled an excuse for the spidery red letters that crawled across the page in crooked sentences. but i nodded to manny, hoping he would understand.

for all its many faults, i had given my story a title. wrote bold across the page, *the stars at oktober bend*. i held gram's torch while manny read.

once there was a greatmother and a greatfarther that took care of the boy called joey and the girl called alice because the other farther was dead and the other mother flew away. the greatmother and greatfarther and joey and alice all lived together up in the sky where the stars and other shiny things were very close and on the ground under the sky was the garden that the greatmother made by putting magic pills in the dirt and the greatfather played music and sang songs. when alice was number twelve she was sitting on the very small mountain near the garden and she was numbering the stars at oktober bend when the robbers came along and set the world on fire then joey pointed and the greatfarther went fast to the very small mountain and he saw what the robbers had did. the robbers ran to there car and the greatfarther ran home very fast and got his snake gun and went under the bridge. the greatmother lu-la-layed alice in her everlasting arms until she went to hospital because her head and other parts of her were bleeding. then policemen came and said the greatfarther did a very wicked sin and they wanted to take his snake gun away and he said it was with the fishes. and they said he would not be able to live near the shining stars anymore but they did not say anything about the very wicked sin the robbers did to the girl called alice. the greatfarther was allowed to stay home until the judgement day but he was not allowed to run away. they told him that after the judgement day he would have to live in another place that was not called hell but there were no windows and no stars. while he was waiting to go to that place the greatfarther made a hole in the roof of the room where alice sleeped when she was not in the hospital he hammered sticks and nails and maid a window and outside the window he hammered more sticks and nails to make a balkeny. and the greatmother of alice said the girl will fall down from the balkeny and be dead because she carnt fly far away like her mother did. and the greatfarther said i will hammer much more sticks so she carnt fall. and he did it and when the girl called alice came home she loved her window to the stars and she was never afraid of falling.

when manny finished reading the small red story he said, 'you are gold, alice nightingale. you are truly gold.' and i laughed because now i knew that gold was excellent and also because i had learnt to write much better that i did then. manny laughed too. it is hard not to laugh with someone when their laughter is made out of pure happiness. our voices became part of the deep humming universe. when we came down again we lay on my bed and twined our legs together the way i had once imagined we would on the narrows of the blue couch. and manny looked so beautiful that i told him the legend of lucifer and asked him if that was his real name.

'my mother called me emmanuel,' he said. 'it means god is with us.'

then he leaned close and pressed his lips to mine. i was not sure if he was telling the truth about his name and its meaning, but i was almost certainly fifteen.

45 MANNY

Two Heads One Heart

I went many times to Alice's house in the school holidays. But one night when I was going home, there were two boys leaning against the wall inside the railway waiting room. It was very late and there were no more trains coming or going and no passengers waiting. Only those two boys were there. It was Tilda's half-brother, Lucas Stewart, and Hamish O'Leary, that is who it was. They stopped leaning against the wall when I came in and I could see that it was me they were waiting for. They stood very close to me. So close that I had to stop.

'Where have you been?' That is what Lucas said to me.

I did not think it was a good idea to tell him where I had been, so I said that I had just been out running. O'Leary laughed. It was not a happy laugh.

'As if!' he said.

'Next time you see Joey Nightingale, tell him to keep away from Tilda,' said Lucas.

'But Tilda likes Joey,' I answered.

'Tilda *thinks* she likes Joey,' O'Leary said. 'Her old man's a copper, and he wouldn't want his daughter getting mixed up with scum like the Nightingales.'

'Why don't *you* tell Joey, Lucas?'

It was only a question. I thought that it was a polite question, but Hamish O'Leary did not like what I had asked his friend. He stepped closer to me and grabbed a handful of my shirt. I remembered the dagger and the drops of blood. If it had been a real knife I could have reached around and severed his spinal cord in seconds. I had seen it done. I had been made to watch. His lips curled back like a snarling dog's.

'Listen smart-arse,' he said, 'just tell him, right? And tell him that if he doesn't, it's payback time'

I had still not grown used to asking people for advice. But on this night I knew that I should speak to kind Louisa James. Perhaps if I told her a little more about Alice I would find it easier to ask her whether or not I should be worried about Hamish O'Leary's warning.

'What is it?' Louisa James asked me before I had spoken a word. She was truly gold.

'I am not certain,' I said.

'Then perhaps we can work it out together. Shall I make cocoa?'

My heart felt lighter then, the way it used to when I was a small boy and my mother would hold my hand and say,

'*Two heads one heart, Emmanuel.*' So I told Louisa James.

'There is a girl, the one I told you about a few weeks ago. Do you remember? The one I took home.'

'You mean the one who had a seizure in the railway waiting room?'

I should have said, *Yes, but she is much more than that, Louisa James.* Instead I nodded.

'Her name is Alice.'

'Yes, I remember. And you've met her again since then?'

'I went for a run near the river and she was there,' I said. 'Now I have met her many times.'

'So Alice is a friend now. Good, good.'

'Yes, Alice is my friend,' I said, and in my heart I knew that I was right to tell Louisa James.

'But there's more?'

'Yes, there is more. There are boys from school who say very bad things about her.'

'What sort of things?'

'They use words I cannot say in front of a lady, Louisa James.'

'Do you believe they're true, Manny?'

'I know they are not.'

'Do you know these boys?'

'Yes, I know them. They play in my football team.'

'Are they your friends?'

'I do not want to be friends with them.'

'Because of what they say about Alice?'

'Because of that and other things.'

'What other things, Manny?'

'One of the boys has a step-sister. They want me to tell Alice's brother to keep away from her.'

'Did they say why?'

I could not tell Louisa James what Hamish O'Leary really said, and although I had seen the way he looked at Tilda Cassidy and heard the things he said to her, I would only have been guessing if I said he was jealous of Joey.

'I asked them why and they said her father would not like it.' That is what I told Louisa James.

'Then the father should speak to his daughter. This has nothing to do with you, or those boys. Do you hear me, Manny?'

'Yes, I hear you, Louisa James, but should I tell Joey?'

'Joey?'

'The brother of Alice.'

'It's nothing to do with you. Don't get mixed up in it.'

I did not want to be mixed up in it, but that did not stop me wondering. What revenge was Hamish O'Leary planning to take if I did not do what he said? And who would he take it on?

july

short days
school holidays and sky
the colour of a gun
joey and the dancing girl
in the house
gram dozing
by the fire wheezing
her way through winter
not looking for trouble
in tilda's eyes
manny and me
under them all under
old charlie's table under
the house under
the floorboards under
dusty chandeliers of
spider silk under
a quilt of patches

in the blue painted noah boat
our salvation
in times of flood
two of every creature
female and male
his french knots upon
my pillow
holy pages in my hands
and manny unaware
of the killer in the corner
the colour of july.

in july, manny and me went on a voyage of our own while bear was in the bath. it was joey's turn to wash and brush her. we took manny's music player in the boat. one bud in my ear. one in his. buds that blossomed into songs, not flowers. powerful music that drummed in our ears like breakers crashing. drove us through the storm. we drifted where the four strong winds and currents took us. light fell like god-rays through the cracks in the kitchen floor above us. at the forty-ninth parallel we dropped anchor and listened to a piece of music that my mother played. an exquisite, melancholy melody. i wondered if she had played it to me while i was in her belly. if she knew even then we would be parted. wondered, too, if manny's mother had sung sad songs to him.

i should have waited. but i had told manny secrets, our

legs had tangled in the hills and valleys of my bedding and many times now his lips had touched mine. i imagined that gave me the right to answers to my questions. he sometimes mentioned the people he lived with in the house of windows. kind louisa and bull james. talked about school and football. but i wanted to know more. wanted to hear about things that had touched him and left their mark.

'did your mother leave you?' i asked, still under the spell of the music.

'yes,' he answered, staring over the bow of our boat like he was searching for distant lands.

i should have sensed how close to the rocks we were. should have seen the darkening sky. felt the waves dash themselves against the flimsy sides of our boat. but i did not. i was like post-office-hattie with her cold eyes and sharp questions. i wanted to know why other people's mothers left them.

'was she young and talented? did they tell you not to stand in her way?'

'my mother is dead,' said manny.

words abandoned me. i was ashamed.

i should have known that death was another reason for forsaking. i slid my right hand between the boat's curved ribs and manny's shoulders. held it with my left to make a never-ending circle of arms around him. tried to draw him close but he stayed frozen. stayed where he was, still as teddy's angel.

'i cannot touch you, alice', he said, 'not the way i want to.'

'you said that i was gold, manny.'

'i did and i meant it.'

'it was those boys, wasn't it? you heard the things they called me. but i am not what they say.'

'i do not listen to what they say.'

'then what is it?'

rain sheeted down beyond the stumps of the house. the river gathered speed. manny said nothing for the longest time and i waited, afraid he would tell me he was mistaken; that i was not shining and precious at all, i was dirty and worthless. at last he spoke but not in a voice i recognised.

'my mother was murdered. they all were. my whole family,' he said in an elsewhere voice that seemed saved for telling unsayable truths. there was no forgetting in manny james, no short-circuiting electrics, no learning again to speak and write. every awful second of what had happened was stamped clear in his mind.

'in my country, the soldiers did terrible things to girls and women. that is what they did to my mother and sister. i was there. they made me watch. i cannot forget. and now when i close my eyes, i see you too, alice. i see you when you were twelve, what those men did to you.'

manny's tears fell, and i howled with rage, 'may they all rot in hell!'

when my throat was raw and our tears had dried to salt, i

whispered, 'don't let them hurt you, too, manny. let us not look back. let us see only what is here and now.'

at last manny's arms went around me. we lay in the belly of the boat, seeking refuge from ourselves and for ourselves in each other. our bodies fit together, soft and hard, giving, taking. and i shed twelveness like a skin.

that night i opened my book of flying and began to write a story: the true story of a boy called emmanuel james and a girl called alice nightingale.

'the peaches were pink as angel's cheeks,' i wrote, 'when manny james began to love alice.'

all i had written there before was mostly longings, wonderings or imaginings; shining things to keep the dark at bay. these new words hungered me for things i had never dared want. what might become of us, i wondered? would love and peaches be enough to satisfy our hunger and make us whole again?

the game

spring was the usual time for big rains in bridgewater, but july rained steady for a fortnight. on the last saturday of the school holidays ribbons of sun, pale as old straw, leaked through the morning clouds, lit my window and seemed like a foretelling of better things. bear pulled her feather-boa tail close. stayed where she was at my feet. i pulled the blankets to my chin, pressed my back to the chimney. downstairs joey made morning sounds: filled the kettle, dumped wood on the hearth, stoked the stove.

when the chimney heated up, i went down, kissed gram and cooked a tower of pikelets. we gobbled them like a celebration of the sun, sprinkled with sugar and squeezed lemon juice. afterwards we carted barrow-loads of firewood from under the house to the verandah. joey stopped when tilda appeared, bright as a robin. red-coated, black-booted.

'we're going to the footy,' joey said.

'football?' i couldn't remember joey ever going to a match before.

'i only go to make dad happy,' tilda said. 'why don't you come with us, alice? you should see manny, he's a star. heaps better than anyone else on the team.'

gold, manny was gold, of course he was! he and i had only ever been together in my world. i wanted to see him in his. did i dare? the bombers would be on the field. i would be only one in a crowd of many spectators. no one would know i was there, i told myself.

'how long does it take to play a game of football?' i asked.

'not too long,' answered joey.

'what about gram?' i asked, but perfect tilda had thought of everything.

'i brought this,' she said, opening the flaps of a cardboard box. 'it's a vaporiser.' she showed us how to fill the reservoir with water. where to put the drops of eucalyptus oil. 'then you plug it into an electricity outlet and it makes steam. it might help your grandma breathe.' then she looked at me like she could tell i was worrying about something. 'don't worry, no one will know it's missing,' she said. 'i used to get croup when i was a kid, but we haven't used it in years.'

we set the steamer going, stoked the stove. i put my arms into my raincoat and my feet into two pairs of socks, and wondered exactly how much nightingale business tilda knew. then i thought about manny and the things i had told him, and for a breath i thought it would be easier if it were just me and joey again. when our love for each other was enough.

we can never go back to that, alice nightingale, because now we have secrets from each other. i did not know how to name the feeling inside me. i could not tell if it was fear or sadness or excitement, or a mixture of all three.

by the time we left, the sun had gone again. joey rode his bike through the drizzle with tilda on the handlebars and me on the parcel rack thinking about manny.

tilda had free passes for her and joey. bear and me got in under the fence behind the visitors' change room. i hurried to where the others stood near a fire drum just around from the goals at the foundry end of the ground. we waited for the teams to run on. the home team jogged onto the field first. striped with black and red, like tilda. they kicked the ball to one another and passed it with their hands. high and low, quick and slow. practising.

'i can't see manny,' joey said.

'maybe he's starting on the bench,' said tilda.

'why would they start their best player on the bench – unless he's not fit?'

a man was standing near us, warming his hands at the fire. he heard joey and tilda talking.

'manny james is on loan to the opposition today. they're three men down.'

'why would the bombers let manny go?' asked joey.

the man shrugged his shoulders. 'they reckon it was captain's choice.'

'which captain?' asked tilda.

'bombers of course. they don't have to do it, but the cheetahs are struggling this season – can't field a team most weeks and haven't won a game since the second round. nice gesture by the bombers, but i dunno why young stewart would give away his best player.'

'he's up to something,' tilda said, after the man had walked off towards the bar.

'what do you mean?' joey asked.

'lucas wouldn't do anything to help another team, i know he wouldn't. he was awarded best and fairest three seasons in a row. but then manny came and he's so much better than everyone else. i think lucas is jealous of him.'

'even if he is, it doesn't explain why he'd loan manny to the cheetahs.'

i heard but didn't understand. football was a mystery to me. then tilda said something that caught my attention. it wasn't her words but the way she said them.

'unless…' she said, then she shook her head and looked at joey. 'oh god, i hope they don't do anything stupid.'

'they?'

'lucas and hamish.'

'it's a game of footy, tilda, there's umpires out there – and rules. they can't just do whatever they like.'

'what are you talking about?' i said. my chest tight.

'it's not important,' joey said. 'look, they're tossing the coin. the game will start in a minute. i s'pose you'll be barracking for the yellow and blacks!'

'for manny,' i said.

i didn't care who won or lost. it was only manny that i watched. his limbs seemed unhinged like a cat's. he moved with grace and strength and speed. at times he soared above the others to catch the red ball in the wide grey sky. though he was dressed in yellow and black, even the bridgewater supporters gasped at the sight of him.

halfway through the game the players left the ground. tilda, joey and me went to the canteen and bought hot sausages and onions wrapped in bread. we ate them with our backs to the fire drum and licked sauce off our fingers.

the players came outside again and the umpire in his long socks and shorts. the ball was tucked under his arm. a silver whistle dangled from a cord around his neck. i remembered what joey said. there are rules and there are umpires. players cannot do whatever they please. i told myself this meant that nothing bad could happen to manny.

the game was almost at its end. the umpire bounced the ball. i watched it rise and fall. saw it spill out between the cheetahs' legs. hands reached in, passed the ball to other hands. fast as lightning to a boot it fell, and i looked from it to manny who leapt above them all. sky was in his hair and on his shoulders as he grasped the flying prize. his hands closed around it. kept it safe and pulled it down with him. down through the cheers until his boots touched the green.

his arms held up the trophy for all to see. from the corner of my eye i saw a movement. an arm raised high and late. too late.

o'leary's arm. down he brought it like a sledgehammer on the back of manny's head. the siren sounded. manny slumped and fell forward onto the field. could not stand up to take his kick. two men in white jackets raced across the ground, looked into manny's eyes, slid a stretcher underneath him and carried him to the changing rooms. i didn't see the umpire give the ball to another cheetah player. didn't see the ball slew sideways from his boot, bounce across the sodden grass, over the boundry line far from the goal. didn't see the umpire turn o'leary around, write down the black number, stitched to his back, on a pad that he took from his pocket. didn't care that the bombers had won by the smallest of margins.

i turned my back on it all. ran to the gate to meet the stretcher-bearers. joey and tilda behind me. i made myself look at manny's head to see if it was split open. there was no blood on him, only mud and blades of grass stuck to the bottoms of his boots where his feet, so fast and graceful, had touched the ground. manny james looked perfect, but his eyes were closed and i wanted him to open them, to look at me and say in his proper way, *alice nightingale, i am so glad that you are here today.* and I wanted to answer, *you were gold, manny james. pure gold.*

but manny didn't open his eyes or speak and i wanted to

cry out, *is there anyone here who knows about acquired brain injury?* fear fastened my tongue and we could only watch as they rushed him by.

family could go inside, they said. and we were not, so we waited at the door in the mud and the drizzle while other people went in and out. the bombers were still in the centre of the ground with their arms around each other's shoulders, singing a song about themselves as though they were gold. but when they reached the gate in the fence, tilda was waiting for the captain.

'you planned this, lucas!' she hissed at him. 'i know you're jealous of manny but you're too gutless to do anything yourself, so you got your stupid mate o'leary to do it for you.'

'i dunno why you're all worked up,' her step-brother said. 'it's only a game of football.'

'you're right about that. it is only a game and there's no place in it for thugs.'

'careful, tilda,' her father said, as he waited outside the clubroom door for his players to file through.

o'leary swaggered close. 'listen to your daddy, sweet-heart, and by the way, what's a lady like you doing, hangin' around with trash?' he turned towards joey and me. cleared his throat and spat on the ground in front of us. then he laughed.

perfect tilda was even more perfect than i thought.

quick as a heartbeat, she landed a right hook. o'leary's nose went sideways and blood sprayed everywhere. i could have hugged her.

48 MANNY

A Little Reminder

'You have a concussion, Manny.' It was the worried face of Louisa James that I saw first when I opened my eyes. Bull was beside her. They came to every game. On fine days, Bull reversed the tray of his utility in close to the fence and they sat on deck chairs in the back and ate sandwiches and drank tea at half-time. Bull boasted that his utility was a grandstand on wheels.

'You should have seen Lou run onto the ground when she saw you go down, son,' Bull said.

I opened my eyes again and saw the honour board that hung on the wall above Bull's head. His name was there, painted in golden letters.

'She ran that fast I reckon the Bombers should recruit her,' he said.

The smile on Louisa's mouth did not match her eyes. I wanted to ask her what had happened, but my lips would not move. The golden letters floated away and I felt myself falling again. Floating and falling, that is what it felt like when I was lying on the stretcher with all those people looking at me.

When I opened my eyes again I was in bed in the house of windows and there was only Louisa James looking at me. She was sitting in a chair beside me. It was dark outside. Clouds passed in front of the moon and small branches scraped at the glass walls of the house.

'Go back to sleep,' whispered Louisa James. When my alarm rang at 6.30, she was still there.

'No running and no school. At least for a couple of days,' she said. 'Stay there and I'll make you a drink.'

It was raining again and I thought about the boat under the house at Oktober Bend and about Alice. Any other Sunday I would have gone to see her. Would she wonder why I had not come? I hoped she believed me when I told her that I took no notice of the things that Lucas Stewart and Hamish O'Leary said about her.

I had not told her how they had stopped me in the railway station waiting room and told me to warn Joey away from Tilda. That was something she did not need to know. Louise James said it was none of my business either and I believed her then. But things were different now. I knew that something was very wrong but I could not remember what it was. I sat up and put my feet on the floor. That is when the walls seemed to move. I began to shiver and sweat dripped off my face. I knew I had been hit in the head and I remembered falling down. Then I remembered what

Hamish O'Leary said to me before his fist connected with my skull. That is when I vomited on Louisa James's shining floor.

In the afternoon, I could sit and stand without feeling dizzy, so I went down to the living room. I did not want to stay upstairs by myself, trying to decide what I should do about Hamish O'Leary and about Alice. It was not a good thing to think about by myself. I sat down at the table and Louisa James sat opposite me. That is where she sat when she wanted to look at me properly.

'How are you feeling?' she said.

'My head is not spinning now,' I said. Louisa James was very good at knowing when I lied.

'That boy O'Leary won't get away with what he did to you,' she said.

A few weeks not playing football, I thought, but what about the other thing he threatened to do?

'Bull's very proud of you, Manny, but it wouldn't break his heart if you didn't want to keep playing.'

I remembered the honour board at the club rooms. Five times Bull's name was painted on it, for the five times he was the Best and Fairest player of all the Bridgewater Bombers. The three true sons of Bull James were not golden boys of football. They were best and fairest at other things; banking and business and medicine.

I played the game because it made Bull happy.

Louisa James's voice was gentle, but I did not want to talk about football. I did not want to think about Hamish O'Leary or what he had said. I wanted to talk about Alice. The sound of her name in the bright warm room would make everything right. That is what I was thinking when Louisa James put aside the peas she had been shelling. She reached across the table and put her hand over mine and that is when I thought I was in trouble.

'Manny,' she said, 'at the game yesterday, there were some young people waiting at the gate when you were carried off the field. They seemed very upset. I thought they might have known you.'

'Was there a dog, a very big dog?'

'I'm not sure,' she said. 'I was so worried about you that I didn't notice much else. All I can remember now is that one of those people was a girl with beautiful hair. Reddish and curly. Very long.'

'Alice,' I said, 'it must have been. Red is the colour of Alice's hair.'

'I wondered if it might be her. Perhaps you should ring and tell her you're okay.'

'There is no phone at Alice's house,' I said. I wanted to hear her voice more than anything else.

'Oh well, I guess you'll see her at school in a couple of days.'

'Alice is not a student,' I said. 'Not at Saint Simeon's,' I said that part quickly and then I kept talking because I had made a mistake.

'She is very clever, Louisa James. She is called The Fly-maker of Bridgewater and she makes trout lures that are so beautiful that some people collect them the way other people collect paintings or other valuable objects.'

I had read those words in a fishing magazine that Joey showed me and I learnt them by heart. Once I started telling Louisa James about Alice, I could not stop.

'Even the labels that Alice makes for her lures are very beautiful. Alice herself made the paper and she draws all the lettering and pictures with a pen dipped in ink. That is what she does.' I wished I could have shown Louisa James the things that Alice made. Then I remembered the poems. I reached into my pocket and pulled out the two I carried with me.

'She also writes poetry,' I said, and I pushed them across the table. Louisa James read the first one.

'I don't know much about poetry,' she said, 'but this is lovely.' Then she picked up the seed packet and I watched her face as she read.

'They're very good,' she said, 'but this one seems so… sad for a girl so young. How old is she?'

'Almost sixteen.'

Louisa James read the poem again. Her face was serious.

'What did you say her name was?'

'Alice.'

'No, I mean her other name.'

Louisa James knew many of the people who lived in Bridgewater; some she had helped into the world, others she had nursed back to health when they were ill. *If I tell you that Alice is a Nightingale, you might remember holding the hand of a young man as he lay dying, and you might know the name of the old man who caused his death.*

That is what I was thinking while Louisa James was looking at Alice's poems. I should have trusted her. She had given a new home and a new life to a boy who had done many wrong things. I should have known that a person who does such things does not judge other people. But before I could speak, my phone began to ring. I took it from my pocket and stared at it, wondering who might be ringing me. It was not the coach and it was not Bull James, *mover of mountains*, and Louisa James was sitting in the same room as me.

'Aren't you going to answer that?'

'Hello?' I said, and I thought I heard the sound of coins falling.

'Hello? Manny? It's me...Joey. Hold on a minute...'

'Manny?'

'Alice?'

'Are you okay?'

Joey had taken Alice to the phone box outside the post

office. When their coins ran out, I switched my phone off and put it in my pocket. My heart was beating very fast.

'It was Alice,' I told Louisa James. 'It *was* her you saw at the game.'

'What's wrong, Manny?'

'She just rang to see if I was all right.'

'What is it you're not telling me?'

'It is nothing,' I said, but Louisa James knew that it was not nothing.

'At the game yesterday, they stopped play while the stretcher was being brought out and I ran onto the ground. The O'Leary boy said something to you and I'm sure he wasn't apologising. Did you hear him? Do you remember what it was, Manny? Is what he said worrying you?'

I shook my head. That is when the table began to slide into the floor. I gripped it tightly and closed my eyes.

'Never mind,' said Louisa James. 'It might come back to you later.'

I could not tell her that it never went away. I could not tell her that I could hardly think of words to speak to Alice on the phone because of what O'Leary said.

'That was a reminder,' he had hissed in my ear. 'Tell Nightingale to keep away from Tilda, soldier boy, or somethin' nasty will happen to his sister.' That is what he said.

49 ALICE

mountain climbing

tuesday morning. undressed birches tapped their bony fingers on my stick-and-nail balcony. it rained all night and still it rained. even with my window closed i heard the low growl of the river swelled wide. scraping its belly over rocks, surging through sedge, bulrush and willow, gobbling wrens' nests from drowning melaleucas. the chimney bricks had lost their heat. the window panes were pearly with breath that escaped me in my dreams. i drew a crooked heart on the misted glass, speared it with cupid's dart. wrote manny's name and mine inside. cleaned another pane with the sleeve of my pyjamas. looked down on the yard all runnied and silvered with slip. a door slammed, the house shook. joey's feet flew fastly up the shuddery stairs and there he suddenly was, his blue-fingered hand on the brass knob of the far flung door, dripping all over my floor.

'the river's over the elephant rocks,' he said, his hasty breath hot in the shivery room. 'c'mon, we gotta get the boat out, just in case.'

bear watched through the screen door while joey pulled
the winch cable out as far as it would reach into the yard.
we picked our way, careful as tomcats, across the slippery
ground till we reached the river end of the house where the
boat was kept. i fetched the book of kells and the cadbury's
roses tin.

joey filled a plastic garbage bin with water
lowered the propellor of the outboard
motor into the bin
opened the choke
primed it
pulled the cord and swore
when it didn't start
did it all
over again exactly
like old charlie did
including the swearing.

joey left the motor idling. fetched the snake gun. wrapped
it in rags and plastic. tucked it in the boat, careful as you
would a baby. killed the motor, lifted it in beside the gun,
pulled a tarp over everything. fastened it tight, knotted a
rope with a truckie's hitch. wedged two steel pipes under
the bow and rolled the boat forward till the pipes were at
the stern. shifted the pipes from back to front till the boat
was close enough to attach the cable hook. we took turns
to wind the slippery winch handle. hauled the boat across

the wet clay yard, up the steps and onto the verandah. padlocked it to a post with a length of chain.

i kicked off my mud-caked boots at the wash-house door. hung my sopping coat to drip dry. joey sat on the step towelling his hair.

'you can have first shower,' he said. 'i'll get the fire going.'

i stayed. sat beside him.

'what are we going to do about gram?' i said. 'what if the rain keeps up? she can't even walk up the stairs. how will we get her out?'

joey stared into the drizzle. quiet. i thought he was going to be mad at me for nagging about gram. finally he opened his mouth.

'ever felt like you were right on the edge of something big, alice? like you're clinging to the side of a cliff, you've done all the hard work, your fingernails are busted, your guts are red raw, your knees are bleeding, but you're so close that all you have to do is throw your leg over the top. then you hear a voice and you look up and someone's beaten you to it. you meet their eyes and you think they're gonna give you a hand, but instead they stomp all over your fingers and turn their back as you fall, and you know that no matter how many times you pick yourself up and climb that rock face, the same thing's gonna happen.'

i had never heard joey talk that way before. never heard him say that many words together. my little brother was always the one who made me feel good. made me feel like i could do anything. i didn't know what to say. writing was easier for me than talking. it gave me time to find the proper words. put down the things i felt. made me understandable. i felt twelve all over again, squatting beside joey, squeezing the wet brown hems of my pyjama pants, trying to find the right words.

'what about tilda?' i said. 'tilda is a very good thing.'

'she won't come no more,' joey said.

then i understood his black mood.

'why not?'

'i went to see her, yesterday, after school. her brother and o'leary bailed me up, said her old man warned her to keep away from me. she won't come back, alice. she can't, even if she wants to.'

was this forsaking? would other people forsake us too? not just family? i thought of tilda in her red coat, bright as poppies in our winter garden. kind tilda with an invitation for me and a vaporizer for gram. brave tilda with her true words and perfect right hook.

'she will come, joey,' i said and i believed. but joey shook his head.

'there's always someone who thinks we're not good enough.'

i took a shower as hot as i could stand it. lightning fanged, the sky rattled. i sat on the broken orange tiles. wrapped my arms around myself and cried for joey. i had found ledges of safety. small pockets of happiness had blossomed on my rock face: a kiss, a kindness, a rare comeuppance. with these i was content. each step was a triumph. i'd never imagined arriving at the top. never wondered if someone waited there. to help me up. or tread my fingers into the dirt. now i wondered if manny's people waited there.

i remembered the strangeness in manny's voice on sunday. but for joey, i would never have gone to the phone box. i hated telephones. the person on the other end could not see me. ears were all they had and ears could not hear the movements of my mouth or the straining tendons in my neck. ears had no way of knowing of my fight to break the silence. joey fed coins into a slot and dialled the numbers. then manny spoke and all the shining queens and kangaroos tumbled in the darkness. the phone was in my hand, waiting, empty and i had to find words for manny. and he for me. when he spoke he did not sound like the boy who had listened to my secrets and told me his.

at the end of our awkward conversation, i knew a little more and a lot less. and now, because of that, i wondered if someone had seen me at the match.

watching manny fly
watching him fall
and me
running and running to

the low latched gate to
the stretcher where he lay with
my arms not around him and
his eyes not looking
did they hear my broken voice cry out,
'does anyone know…?'
did they?

did they tell manny james to keep away from me? or was he more broken than he told me on the phone? because now it was tuesday and still he had not come.

joey was in the kitchen when i came to get dressed in front of the fire. gram was as gray as the clay in the yard and felt the same – cold and damp. there was just us three again and we did what we had to do.

joey said, 'you gotta walk, gram, else your lungs will drown.'

'so you think you're a doctor now?' she wheezed.

'i looked it up at school,' he said, 'c'mon.'

we upped her from her cot, together again, the way we were before tilda and manny. me under one shoulder, joey under the other. this was our rock face, our nightingale business.

'river's up,' joey said.

'think i can't hear it?' said gram, sliding her knitted

slippers along the floor like she was skiing across the forty-ninth parallel.

'we got the boat ready, gram,' i said.

'me and charlie used to go fishin' in that boat.'

'maybe when you're better we can go again. you, me and joey.'

'that's enough,' she said and stopped. 'i'm all out of breath.'

'once more,' joey said and we lumped her round the kitchen again, slow as a month of wet sundays.

gram leaned herself against the sink to catch her breath. i brushed her hair slow and smooth while we stared out. behind the orchard where our bonfires once burnt, the river spread her creamy petticoats. i wondered if gram was remembering old charlie pulling me and joey in the billy cart, wheeling our homemade angel to her fiery death. wondered if her superstitious mind believed that burning the angel had let to all our troubles, to cliffs that none of us could climb.

my fingers parted her hair into tributaries and streams. wove them under and over and under again. tied the ends with a scrap of wool and wound the finished braid around her head like a crown. fastened it with bobby pins.

'you look like a queen, gram,' i said. it was ten o'clock and the smell of frying eggs was in the air. i held a mirror to her face, but she pushed it away.

'who's that i see comin' through the orchard?' she said.

joey left the eggs and me and gram. and he, not yet showered, barefoot and still in pyjama shorts, magicked himself across the muck without a slip to unlatch the orchard gate. inside me and gram laughed to see him, nearly naked in the pouring rain, holding the pickets so gentlemanly for the girl he thought would never come.

50 ALICE

precious

only the tips of the garden gate's pointed pickets were visible on wednesday morning. looked like a dinosaur's back zig-zagging through the muddy water. half a dozen red hens roosted on the kitchen windowsill. we could almost have dived off the verandah at the river end of the house. the other end was built on bedrock. we could have climbed out the window and stepped onto the ground there.

'we'll be fine,' joey said, 'the distance between the floor and the water's gotta be at least two metres, and anyway, it's stopped raining now.'

i didn't feel fine. 'what if it starts again?'

'i'll come home. promise. the boat's ready now, all we gotta do is get gram onboard. don't worry.'

joey went to school and i fed the hens leftover porridge that i couldn't eat because now it was wednesday and still manny had not come. i built a newspaper hen's nest in the bottom of the boat, washed the dishes and stoked the fire.

after i bathed gram and helped her change her clothes, i went upstairs. put all my papers, labels and the book of flying in plastic bags.

gram went to sleep after lunch and i opened the dresser drawer and searched amongst the shoelaces and string, the blackout candles, the deck of cards, the matches, torch and rubber bands. found papa's metal tape-measure and four new batteries. stuck the end of the tape through a knothole in the kitchen floor and measured the distance between the floor and the water. it was still more than two metres and it wasn't raining. maybe joey was right. maybe we'd be fine. i took the radio off the mantelpiece. searched for spiders in the sleeves of my raincoat and filled its pockets with everything i needed. then bear and me went walking.

the river track was under water so we took our secret route to the railway station. the way i had showed manny. when we passed the place where i had held back the fence, i remembered how manny held my hand and would have taken me with him. but his world was not mine. not then and not now. maybe not ever. we followed the fence along the road until we came to the place where the couch fell from the back of a truck, tumbled to the edge of charlotte's pass and buried its silver casters in the weeds.

the soupy river swelled out below me. it had guzzled the rope above the tarpit and the limb from which it hung. but the barbecue, the concrete picnic table and teddy's memorial were still well above the water. i slid down the slippery sheep trails. bear followed, nimble as a mountain goat. i wrenched out tufts of grass and dead thistles from beside the angel's feet. scraped and scrabbled with my hands, burrowed like a rabbit in the dirt, down amongst the living things, roots and worms and memories. my nails were torn.

my fingers stung where thistle spines pierced them. but there was nothing to be found. nothing left. there couldn't be. i knew that.

i turned the radio on. took the chisel from my raincoat pocket and the tack hammer that old charlie used when he banged new heels on our worn out boots. began to chip carefully at the soft sandstone under the angel's feet. three o'clock came quickly. news headlines then the weather report. i did not need to be told more rain was coming. gunmetal clouds parachuted onto the hills. i stood back to look at my finished work and suddenly there came manny, rushing downhill like the wind.

'alice!' he said. 'i've been everywhere looking for you. i was worried. what are you doing down here?'

i stared at him. at his face, his head, wanted to make sure he was okay after what o'leary did. wanted him to smile at me. he did not. manny saw the tools in my hand. then his eyes went to the letters i'd marked on the stone. he looked for a long time. then knelt and traced the letters with his fingers.

'precious nightingale,' he said softly. 'was there a baby, alice?'

'i don't know,' i said. 'no one can tell me. gram said little girls don't have babies. but what if she's wrong? what if there was? if it existed at all, for a day or an hour, it shouldn't be forgotten, should it?'

51 ALICE

in which manny has come to warn me and joey

lightning split the southern sky. gram's radio spat and crackled. i put it inside my coat. manny grabbed my tools.

'home, bear, home!' i yelled above a thunderclap. she stayed close as we ran. constant companion, never forsaking, not even in a storm.

clouds gutted themselves on the radio tower behind the fire station. the first fat drops spat at our heels as we reached our hole in the fence. i ran faster, heart thumping, feeling guilty, needing to be home. to measure by eye the distance between river and floor. stopped when i saw the house was safe, a peninsula of land still surrounding it.

manny grabbed my hand, held me back.

'before you go inside, is there somewhere private we can talk? just you and me?'

'i should go in to gram...'

'joey and tilda are with your grandmother. i came here first when i was looking for you. please, alice, there is something important i must tell you.'

the rain was pouring now. we needed to find shelter quickly. 'under the house?' i said, hoping it was still dry up the high end. manny nodded.

i spread my raincoat on the ground. manny's eyes lit on me for a moment, as if to measure whether i could bear the weight of what he had to tell me. then we huddled together, shivering. heads almost touching the wooden beams above us. bear shook her coat, flung water everywhere, then curled up close to me.

i heard joey's muffled footsteps and faint voices in the kitchen at the other end of the house. when manny spoke, his voice was almost a whisper. 'there are things i should have told you before,' he said, and my stomach coiled like clock springs. 'in my country, i watched soldiers burn villages and murder and torture people. i saw my mother and sister bleeding on the ground and i did nothing to help them. when everything i had was gone, the soldiers kept me safe. when i did as i was told, they gave me food and cigarettes. then they gave me a gun. if they had ordered me to kill a man, i think i would have. i was ten years old and i was like them, a soldier.'

anger exploded inside me. i wanted to shout. not because manny had told me things i didn't want to know, but because they had happened. did he think holding a gun made a boy a soldier? did he think being raped made a girl a whore?

'do you think this will change the way i feel about you?' i whispered. *do you think it will stop the skip of my heart when i see you? do you know why papa is in jail? do you think what he did made me love him any less?*

'i was wrong not to tell you,' he said. 'you deserve to hear it from me, not from someone else.'

people do not speak to me, emmanuel. only you *tell me things you do not want to say. only* you *listen.* 'who else knows?' i said, 'louisa james?'

'louisa james knows almost everything about me, that is true. but she would never tell anyone else. that is not the kind of person she is.'

'who then? please, not joey.'

'no, it is not joey.' manny shook his head. 'but i must also speak to him about this.'

'you have told me. that is enough. you are not a soldier. and my brother doesn't need to know everything about his sister,' i said, suddenly glad manny shared his past with me before others changed his history into something it was not.

'i must tell him,' manny said again, and i saw his troubled eyes. was this what gram had seen?

'what's wrong, manny?' i said.

'the person who found out about the things i did, says i must tell joey not to see tilda anymore, and if i do not, someone will get hurt.'

'you mean mister cassidy? tilda says her father said nothing. she says o'leary's a liar for telling joey that.' manny's expression did not change.

'now that i have told you,' he said, 'it doesn't really matter who else knows what i did before i came to bridgewater. but it is not the coach who found out. and even if it was, it is not me that i am worried about, or joey. and that is the truth, alice.'

'i don't understand.'

i crept an arm around his shoulder and leaned my head against his chest. the knitted stitches of his damp jumper pressed plain and purl patterns on my cheek. beneath them beat the steady rhythm of manny's heart.

'tell me everything, manny.' his arms closed me in.

'alice, there is someone who might hurt you.'

'hurt me? who might hurt me?'

'it is hamish o'leary. he said that something would happen to you if joey did not stop seeing tilda. that is why i have to talk to joey. that is what i have to tell him. that is why hamish punched me at the game. so that i would know that he was serious.'

i had seen the way hamish o'leary looked at tilda. it was clear why he wanted joey to stop seeing her. but i didn't understand why he had threatened to harm me, not joey.

'when did he tell you this?'

'at the football match.'

'when he hit you. i saw him say something to you.'

manny nodded. 'so you see, i must tell joey.'

'you can't, manny.'

'but he loves you, alice, and...'

'that's why you can't tell him. he's already done enough for me. i'm going inside now. you can come with me but you can't say anything to joey.'

52 ALICE

the o'leary question

joey saw us coming. met us on the verandah, furious. i'd been away too long. gram had pissed in her bed and cried because she'd done it. i cried when joey told me. cried for gram because she was old and now her waterworks were buggered as well as her lungs, and because i hadn't been there to help her out of bed onto the bucket and wipe her bum and tuck her in. i cried because i could tell the river was higher without sticking papa's tape measure down the hole, and because i knew joey was worried. and maybe just a little bit because of what hamish o'leary said to manny.

'i am sorry,' manny said. 'it was my fault. there was something important i had to tell alice.'

'it's just possible that our house might float down the river sometime in the next forty-eight hours – what's more important than that?'

'i am sorry, joey, i really am,' manny said.

i wiped my face on my sleeve. glared at manny, afraid he

was going to tell joey about o'leary. tilda saved me.

'let them come inside, joey. you must be freezing,' she said linking her arm through mine. joey breathed out. calmed down.

gram called out, 'what are you all doing, standing around out there? come inside. what's a woman have to do around here to get a cup of tea?'

'i've told her we might have to leave,' joey said. 'she won't hear of it. see what you can do, alice.'

'we'll put the kettle on,' said tilda, 'come on, manny.'

'how bad is it really, joey?' i asked.

'emergency services say it should peak around mid-night. they're predicting we'll be safe here at bridgewater. but i think we should all to be ready to go, just in case. it's just after 6.30 now, so we should have plenty of time.'

tilda was sitting on the table doing something with her phone. manny was pouring tea.

'manny and i have invited ourselves to stay here tonight,' tilda announced. 'because we've got phones and you might need them. i just let dad know i'm staying at a friend's house,' she said.

joey and i made scrambled eggs on toast for everyone. when gram finished i said, 'i'll put some warmer clothes on you.' i rubbed her back with vicks, zippered old charlie's fleecy fishing jumper over her nighty, pulled on two pair of socks and tracksuit pants over the top.

'that's enough,' she grumbled, 'i'll get too hot.'

'we might have to leave the house later on and go somewhere safer, gram. they say there's a lot of water coming down.'

'they don't know what they're talking about. i've never seen the river flood in july.'

'best to be ready, just in case,' i said. tucked her in tight.

while gram dozed we packed our precious things
in plastic bags
photographs of daddy and us
on his knees
and in the air above
his strong brown
arms and
smiling face.
the dictionary full
of words and
gram's bible
lures and labels
pens and nibs and inks and pages
empty and full and the tea
caddy bank.

upstairs we went. arms laden with small treasures. bear and me stayed behind, a moment longer than the others. i opened my window out into the dripping, moonless dark. saw the river run by, fat and black as molasses. slammed the panes together hard and ran down. ran everywhere. flicking switches, turning lights on, making our small world brighter, safer. safe with gram snoring and the fire burning and the radio playing weather reports, emergency bulletins and the 8.30 news of places near and far away.

'let's play truth or dare,' i said when news of the world was finished and we knew the temperature in rome and in paris and madrid. i didn't want to think about how close the river was to the floor of the house for the next five hours or however long it took before we knew if we were going to be safe or not.

 'yeah, let's do it,' tilda said.

 'want to have a look outside first?' joey asked.

 'not me,' i said.

 'me either,' said tilda.

 'i'll come,' manny said.

joey lit a hurricane lantern and he and manny went outside onto the verandah. tilda, bear and me watched from inside. light flickered across the endless ocean. bear whined and put her head in my lap. manny took his phone from his pocket.

 'this is manny,' we heard him say. 'is bull there?' bull james was the man who built the house of windows. bull james moved mountains. i'd seen it written on all his tipping trucks and on his yellow caterpillar machines that

235

pushed the rocks of bridgewater around as though they were popcorn. manny talked for a while, then passed his phone to joey. when the conversation was ended, the boys came inside.

'all the reports say that we're in no immediate danger, but bull says he'd like to get us out as soon as possible,' joey explained. 'he says they'll use sandbags to build a breakwater in the shunting yards, so the current's not so strong. then they'll set up a floodlight. once that's been done he'll ring manny and the emergency services rescue boat will come across to get us all.'

'why can't we just go now – in our own boat?' i asked.

'bull's worried the motor's too small. and besides, we'd have to make two trips.'

we began the waiting game. and our game of truth or dare. but no one was very interested because of the creeping water circling us and because we were waiting for manny's phone to ring. when it was my turn to ask joey a question, he chose truth. i couldn't think of anything interesting to ask, so i said, 'what are the names of the boys who got killed on the bridge?'

joey didn't answer straight away. everyone went quiet, waiting for him to say something.

'what difference does it make who they were?' he said.

'nobody ever told me who they were. i just want to know.'

'this is supposed to be a game, alice, not a bloody inter-
rogation!' he laughed awkwardly. looked embarrassed.

'tell me, joey.'

'geez, alice, this is family business. ask me about it later.
not here, not now.'

'i need to know now. it might be important.'

'what do you mean?'

'just tell me.'

'what's it matter who the bastards were? what difference
does it make now?'

'i have a right to know.'

joey kicked his chair back. it clattered to the floor. bear
sprang to her feet. came to heel beside me. joey ignored
her. strode across to the sink and stared out the window into
the blackness. silent seconds ticked by before my brother
spoke to his reflection in the window.

'it was joel ellis,' he said.

'and the other one?'

'liam. his name was liam.'

'liam who?'

i was ready this time. no ravens, no cross-wired
electricals. just me wanting to make sense of my past, my
present and my future. joey spun around to face me.

'shit, alice, what are you trying to do?' bear's ears lifted.

'i'm not the guilty one.'

manny watched me. didn't try to stop me. joey sat down
beside tilda and put his head in his hands.

'o'leary. it was liam o'leary, hamish's older brother. he was twenty when he and the other bloke…attacked you. old charlie tried to stop them getting away. he fired at the ute. it flipped and went over the bridge. ellis was killed instantly. o'leary's neck was broken and he died in hospital. the car was nicked, they were both over .05 and o'leary never even had a license. if you're looking for the reason why hamish o'leary threatened to hurt you, it's probably because, in some weird twisted way, he thinks it's your fault his brother's dead.'

'you knew?' i said. 'you knew hamish threatened me?'

joey groaned, 'yes, i knew.'

'who told you?'

'he did. he said if i didn't stop seeing tilda, he'd get you.'

my mind spun. joey knew and didn't tell me. knew and yet he still kept seeing tilda. this was too much for me to understand at once.

'look alice…maybe we can talk more about this later. right now there's more urgent things to deal with.'

'no!' said tilda. 'you need to settle this thing now. don't blame joey, alice. you need to hear my side of the story. after manny got hurt, joey thought he should take o'leary's threat seriously. he told me he couldn't see me anymore. said my father warned him off. i didn't believe him because my dad's not like that. you're lucky, joey's the best brother and the best friend anyone could have. it's me you should be mad at, alice. i couldn't keep away from joey even after he confessed that he'd lied to me. and to you. i understand why he did it. but i just want you to know this, alice. joey told me what happened to you when you were twelve. those blokes were cowards and so is hamish o'leary. my dad says that if we let people like them stop us from living the way we want to, we let them win. but i think you already know that, don't you, alice?'

joey disappeared outside and tilda, perfect tilda, went after him. manny and i stared at one another. gobsmacked, dumbstruck. she took my breath away. if we weren't about to be washed away, i think i would have got up on papa's table and danced. in that moment, i felt like i could do almost anything.

then manny's phone rang.

53 ALICE

the traffic on tullamarine freeway

it was 10.50 on thursday night and bull james was on the phone. the emergency services boat had been dispatched. but not to us, bull told manny. to a small town ten kilometres upstream where a car carrying three passengers had been washed off a bridge. we'd have to wait until the boat and crew returned, bull said. he didn't know how long it would take. i shook gram awake. helped her across to her chair by the fire. made coffee.

forty-five minutes later, the rescue boat still hadn't arrived. joey stuck his finger through the knothole in the floor and touched the river.

'shit, where are they?' he said.

bear leaned against my legs and whined. i stroked her ears while manny rang bull and told him about joey's finger in the knothole and the river underneath.

'we can't wait any longer. we're coming in joey's boat,' manny said.

'what's going on?' said gram.

'we're leaving,' i told her. 'the river's nearly up to the floor.'

'not on your nelly,' said gram. 'i'm not going anywhere.'

'you can't stay here, gram. put this on. quick!' i tried to stuff her arms into the sleeves of a waterproof jacket. her arms hung limp and heavy. dressing her was almost impossible.

'i been through floods before. lord jesus will look after me. take me upstairs, nearer my god to thee.'

'you'd never make it upstairs! if you stay here you'll drown.'

tilda came to help. finally, we got the jacket on. gram lay back down on her bed.

'the night air won't do me chest any good,' she said, wheezing. stubborn. maybe scared.

i smelled two-stroke and heard the outboard motor kick in, then die. heard joey swear and try again. looked out the window at the boys up to their knees in water. wished it was possible to tow the whole house to high ground.

we all knew there'd have to be two trips. the plan was to take gram first. joey knew the river better than anyone so he would steer. he needed crew: someone to hold the lantern and watch for hazards that might upend the boat. the other to mind gram. to help keep her calm. make sure she didn't try to stand up or jump out.

'come on, gram. you and papa used to love the boat,

remember?' i tried to coax her. 'we're not going far. it won't take long.'

gram refused to walk. they had to carry her. manny at her shoulders, joey at her feet. her eyes stubbornly shut. tears dribbling down the gullies of her face like a flood of her own was leaking out. i held the door ajar while they took her through.

the motor and the rain both steady now. joey walked down the steps as far as he could without gram's back touching the water. tilda and i held the boat against a verandah post. tried to keep it still while the boys lifted gram over the side. she lay there with her eyes shut, bum and back on the bottom of the boat. knees bent up and over the seat. i pulled off my windcheater to cushion her head. tried not cry on her rained-on face.

'take alice and tilda with you,' manny said.

'the girls aren't strong enough to stop gram if she struggles...if she tries to get out,' joey said.

'you go first, tilda,' i said. 'there'd be no room for bear and i can't leave without her.'

joey didn't argue. handed me the gun.

'keep it here,' my brother said. maybe because it was nightingale business that he didn't want to have to explain to someone at the other side. maybe not. maybe it was to keep me safe. i didn't ask.

'go upstairs when we leave, and stay there till i come back,' joey said.

tilda pressed her phone into my hand. showed me where manny's number was and triple zero. how to make it work.

'i didn't bring my charger, but the phone's been turned off, so here's hoping it will last for a little while.'

she hugged me. then stepped into the boat. cradled gram's head on her knees. gentled the hair away from her forehead maps, carved deep by sickness and sorrow. part of me wished it was me sitting there with joey. bear at my feet, gram's head in my lap. but part of me was glad because manny and tilda felt almost like kin.

manny lifted the lantern down, passed it to tilda. then in front of them all he gathered me close and kissed my lips. joey opened the throttle a little and closed it again, like a polite 'ahem'.

manny whispered, 'my sister was called precious.' then he turned away. stepped into the boat.

he sat on the middle seat beside gram's knees. he was the arms to hold her tight in case she tried to climb out. tilda was the light to show the way and joey was the tillerman to steer them all to the other side. he opened the throttle. the motor turned the tiny propeller. it was like watching an egg-beater in an ocean. i shivered. bear barked into the night. then we ran upstairs.

i stood the gun in the corner of my room. dragged pillows and a blanket to my rain-spattered window. made a nest for me and bear. burrowed into her softness and warmth while we watched tilda's light bob. wondered when i would see it come back again. unpicked the moments before the others left; the looks on their faces, the things they had done, the words they had said. asked myself why manny had chosen that moment to tell me his sister's name. why he hadn't waited until we were safe. all safe. was this another goodbye? was that what manny thought? i slid my thumb inside the blanket's worn satin binding. rubbed my cheek with it, the way i did on the day of my daddy's leaving. the way i had for months of night-times after. tried not to close my eyes. when i did i thought i felt the house move.

the man on the radio said it was 5.45am and city traffic was light on eastlink and on tullamarine freeway, and all lanes were open on the westgate bridge. after that i listened to the news from far away. the announcer didn't mention a town called bridgewater or a flood at oktober bend. he had probably never heard if it. so i took my finger out of the blue blanket satin, turned the radio off and listened to the rain on the roof for a while. when i looked outside again the rain had stopped. the sky behind the slaughter-yards was the colour of a bruise and our house was an island.

'rain before seven, fine by eleven,' i told bear to jolly her. she smiled and we wandered downstairs like we had all day to do it. then up again we sped as fast as lightning strikes. me fumbling for tilda's phone. trying to remember which numbers to press. wishing for a voice in my ear saying *yes*,

244

it's manny here. and him listening while i tell him all the awful things that bear and me have seen.

i cannot poke my finger in the knothole, i would say, *because the lion's feet are off the floor and old charlie's table and gram's bed are almost knock, knock, knocking on heaven's door. traffic is light on eastlink and on tullamarine freeway and all lanes are open on the westgate bridge but where is our little boat, emmanuel? and when is it coming to oktober bend to fetch bear and me?*

but tilda's phone had gone to sleep in the night. the little window stayed black. there were no numbers to press, no voice in my ear, no one to talk to. i took my calm pills and sat on the bed with my arms around bear.

54 MANNY

Sailing Away

Precious is a very good name to give a child, even one you have not held. Especially one you have not held. That is what I should have said to Alice. That is what I was thinking when I was in that tiny boat on the very wide river.

My sister was brave and beautiful. She would not tell the soldiers where our mother was. They raped her and still she would not tell them. That is how brave she was. Then they took her tongue. They laughed and said she would not need it. I left Precious lying on the ground. I left Alice at the drowning house. It was not a proper way to say goodbye. I am the one who left them both. That is who I am.

That is what I was thinking when the light that Bull James promised failed us. There were many clouds that night and we could not see the moon. All that we had was one small lantern. It was not enough to show the way. We could not even see where the river ended and the land began. No one saw what hit our boat. We could not tell what hidden thing had spun us around. It dipped the stern and raised the bow.

The metal tool box slid out from under Joey's seat. The lamp was torn from Tilda's hand and dashed against the seat, and Mrs Nightingale cried out. I shone the light from my phone onto Alice's grandmother, who lay very still in the bottom of the boat. There was a gash on her forehead.

'It looks like she might have hit her head on the tool box,' Tilda said. 'Is there a first aid kit on-board? Joey?'

I held my phone up high. And that is when we saw that only half of Joey was in the boat. His head and shoulders were below the water. I pulled him back into the boat. He coughed many times and then he sucked air into his lungs.

'Get the oars! Quick!' he said. 'The motor's gone, I couldn't hold it. Whatever we hit has ripped it off. We'll have to row.'

'Joey...' said Tilda.

'Help me find the oars.'

Tilda was very stern.

'Shut up and listen, Joey!' she said. 'Your Gram's been hurt.'

I phoned Bull James. It was the only thing to do. The current was too strong to row against.

Bull said it was the wind that brought the light down and smashed it on the railway line. 'Give us five minutes and we should have another one up and running,' that is what he said. I told him that we did not have five minutes. Our motor was gone, oars were useless against the current, an injured lady was lying in the bottom of the boat, and Alice and Alice and Alice...

247

We drifted in the darkness. We could not tell how fast or slow, only that we were moving. I opened my phone again. Ten minutes had passed since I last spoke to Bull. I shone the light on Grandmother Nightingale's face. There was a cut, high up on her forehead. Joey had pinched it shut with his fingers to stop the bleeding. He knelt in the bottom of the boat, talking to his grandmother. She was very pale and was not moving.

'It's all right, Gram, we'll have you home soon.' Joey whispered small lies into his grandmother's ear to comfort her. Then Bull's light came on. It shone a pathway across the water and we could see the thing that hit us. It was a large shed. A hay shed. The walls and the roof and all that was inside it. Sheets of iron, wooden poles and hay. Hundreds of large round bales of hay. Our boat was surrounded by them. My phone rang. This time it was Louisa James.

'This is Manny. I have put you on loudspeaker, Louisa James.'

'We can see you. We've given the SES crew your position and the boat's on its way. Can you hear me, Manny?

'Yes, we can hear you. Please tell them to come quickly.'

'Listen carefully. You've drifted past the breakwater, but that debris you're caught in has really slowed you down. Bull says as long as the mass of bales doesn't disperse, you'll be fine. He's waiting on the bridge with a sling on a crane. If the SES crew doesn't make it before you reach him, he'll lower two men in harness and they'll put a sling around your boat and try to take the whole thing up. Do you understand?'

'Yes. Please tell them to hurry. Tell them Mrs Nightingale is injured and –'

'We know, Manny. An ambulance will be waiting. I have to go now. Bull's on the radio.'

'Wait, Louisa! Alice is not with us.'

'Where is she? What's happened?'

'We could not all fit in the boat. Alice stayed at her house. You must get someone to go there.'

'They'll never stop us if we get past the bridge,' Joey said, and I wished I had stayed with Alice. We might have been safer there. And if we were not, at least we would have been together.

55 ALICE

submarines and sirens

our house was the only one in bridgewater built on the flood plain. gram said there once were others. some had been demolished. some got washed away by other floods. soon there would be none. our place was listing now. leaning to the west. i felt like our house. cast adrift in an unfamiliar landscape.

bear and me went outside. sat together on the balcony that papa made with love and sticks. our tank slid sideways off its stand and floated past the wash-house like a stubby submarine. i thought about the handprints on the concrete, underneath the water. our daddy's and his baby sister's. it was all we had of them, except for a few photographs. who would tell papa when everything was gone? where would we go? where would papa go when it was time for him to come home? i put my arms around bear's neck. tried not to think sad thoughts while we waited for our rescuers to come, or not.

the foundry whistle blew for smoko. startled us. reminded me that life went on as usual for people whose homes weren't on the flood plain.

'oh where, oh where has our little boat gone, dear bear,' i sang to constant companion to comfort her. to cure her of her fear of sirens and submarines. to pass the time.

a tree floated by with a cow, a small cupboard and clothes line caught in its branches. lodged itself on the roof of the wash-house. the drowned cow stared at me over the clothes line. i looked away from her sad brown eyes. down i looked and saw the river, already licking at the sticks and nails put there to keep me safe.

and i
because bear could not climb onto the roof and
because i would not leave her alone and
because i could not think of prayers
or poems
or proper words to say
cried out into the large and empty air
send the bloody boat, god
please, send the bloody boat!

shipwrecked

it drifted, small as pea-pod, on the misty grey horizon.
vanished behind vast tree canopies made to look as small
as bouquets by the floodwater, and i wondered if the boat
i'd seen was only a mirage, a cruel trick, or the memory of
a ghostly boat...

> filled with joy and us
> gram and me and little joey
> with fishing rods and
> red water wings around
> our spindly arms and
> our daddy's safe brown hand
> steady on the tiller
> papa up the pointy end watching
> for submerged snags.

i almost cried for joy when it reappeared. then with dis-
appointment as it came closer. it was a toy, puffed up with

air. a rubber boat to use on long, hot summer days when the river was clear and quiet. wondered what fool had sent that small and orange boat. clearly no match for a river that eddied and swirled, fat with cows, cupboards and clothes lines and whatever else had taken its fancy. despite its egg-beater motor, papa's boat would have been a better choice by far. this plaything might not even hold us all: its captain, bear and me.

but i told myself that any boat was better than none. even this one that sat low in the water and went wherever the river took it instead of charting a course direct to us. i took off my yellow raincoat. waved it madly. the captain raised both his arms in response. crossed and uncrossed them above his head. marked the cold grey sky with giant kisses again and again, until i understood. he had no means of steering. no oars, no motor. he was as helpless as i.

reckless, the boat approached our house. fast, too fast. sucked in by rips and currents that licked and swirled around walls, through smashed windows and flapping doors. bear whined and i held her collar tight, afraid she might leap into the water and swim to meet the boat.

'watch out!' i yelled. but there was nothing the boatman could do. the river spun his craft around, swept it into the wash-house tree. branches pierced the rubber and the dead cow's horns tore it to ribbons. the young man clung to the drowned tree, draped limply as wet washing over limbs and twigs. i saw a tattoo where his neck burst from his shoulders.

a dagger and drops. black drops, drip, dripping down his back with the floodwater. then he turned and looked at me.

into his shipwrecked eyes i stared. he was not a captain, just a boy. a boy who blamed me for the death of his brother. that young man who'd almost killed me.

'why have you come?' i said. brave and stupid. as if he would tell me that. 'i know what you told my brother and manny. that's why you're here, isn't it? to pay me back.'

he looked away. didn't answer. hand over hand, on the leafless white limbs, he moved towards the house, towards me.

'talk!' i yelled. angry he had come now. now when i was alone. now when there was no ground to put my feet on. nowhere to run, nowhere to hide. 'what do you want?' but he said nothing. saved all the fight that was in him to bend his cold blue fingers around the branches and hold tight. the water curled around him, sucking and pulling.

i shortened bear's lead. took her with me through my window. away from the water and o'leary. backed into the room. nudged something in the corner with my elbow. turned and saw the gun. was this why joey had given it to me? in case hamish came? surely my brother wouldn't have left me if he'd thought this might happen. surely he never meant for me to fire the gun?

i backed away from it. my heart thumped, my blood raced and my head spun. then the house moved. the ceiling

254

tilted and my bed began to slide slowly towards the back of the room. i sank to the floor, clung to bear. afraid the birds were coming, that my wires were crossed. she whimpered, nuzzled my neck with her nose. i opened my eyes, saw water seeping beneath the bedroom door. it was real. the house had come undone from its foundations. water was rising inside.

we ran towards the window. flung ourselves through. slammed it shut behind us and huddled together outside. every tiny movement was magnified. i prayed the house would not turn again. would not roll over on its back with its belly in the air and sink. when i dared open my eyes, my window no longer faced along the valley towards the footbridge and charlotte's pass. it jutted up obliquely to the sky like a small observatory. below my little balcony, the wall of the house sloped away into the water. i was afraid to look inside the house. afraid it would be like looking through the side of an aquarium. kept my eyes fixed on the wash-house, on the cow and on the clothes line sailing downstream. felt bear's sides move. felt her belly swell with rage. when i looked down, her ears were flattened to her skull, her lips drawn back, waiting for a word from me. her eyes and mine locked on the shipwrecked boy. clinging to the bottom of the balcony.

'why do you hate me?' i said, hardly knowing i'd spoken out loud. needing to hear it from him. not that it mattered. not if we were both going to drown.

it might have been minutes or hours that we stared at one another. it might have been seconds.

'because i miss him,' groaned hamish, like the words were a confession. his face was pinched, his skin was ash.

grief was in him and in me. it was the price we paid for what others had done.

years after our daddy died, gram said, 'death sets you free. it takes you to a place where there is no pain. no suffering. no grief.'

i heard the timber slat crack. saw it give way in o'leary's hand.

'help me?' he asked like he knew the answer would be no. i was cold, tired and wet. i felt forsaken. hamish's words could have meant anything right then. help me die, help me live, help me forgive or forget. put an end to my grief.

i could have helped him put an end to his grief. there was a loaded gun inside my door. a dog at my side, constant companion, awaiting my command. i could have stomped on his tired hands and watched him float away. no one would ever know what happened. i leaned closer to o'leary, so he could hear what tilda's father said.

'if we let cowards stop us living the way we want to, we let them win. i won't let you win, hamish,' i said.

there's courage and there's caution, gram's voice was in my head. i took bear's lead off. knotted it around the window latch, leaned my back against the wall, braced my feet against the balcony and dropped the looped end to o'leary.

'now pull!' i yelled.

his freezing fingers gripped. the leather strap pulled tight and o'leary dragged himself up the side of the house. collapsed on his stomach and lay there, shivering, shaking.

'you *are* crazy,' he said, when he had breath to speak. 'really crazy. i mean, i could push you overboard. you couldn't stop me.'

it might have been because i was cold, wet, tired and forsaken, but it almost sounded like o'leary meant crazy in a good way.

i nodded at bear. she snarled and bared her teeth.

'i don't think so,' i said. 'and anyway, the boat's coming.'

the rescue crew wrapped us all in shining cloth to make us warm. bright as the stars at oktober bend we were, bear and me and hamish o'leary.

57 ALICE

love letters to gram

amongst the little crowd of faces i saw them: brother joey and my truest friends. emmanuel and perfect tilda. smiled to greet me. reached out to hold me.

an ambulance was waiting. paramedics slid me and hamish in on beds with wheels. a voice i didn't know said, 'medical assistance dog', and bear leapt up beside me.

'we'll meet you at the hospital,' yelled joey before they closed the doors. and only then i saw the empty space.

'where's gram?' i said. 'where's gram?'

'the old lady in the boat,' hamish told them.

'mrs nightingale – she's at the hospital. it's standard procedure after a rescue. once they've checked you over, you can ask to see your grandma.'

at the emergency department, they checked our vital signs. blood and breath and pulse and heart. talked amongst themselves about shock and hypothermia. said that we should stay for observation. hamish in the men's ward. me and bear in with the kids. i was too tired to point out their mistake. to tell them i was twelve no longer.

two nurses took away my yellow raincoat. peeled my sopping pants off and my jumper. tucked me in between the sharp-edged sheets and primrose blanket. plumped the pillows. spooned something sweet onto my tongue to help me sleep. then swished the curtains back, as though they were unveiling something special. better than a work of art, a mona lisa, a marble bust. something rescued from the flood. a girl alive!

when they told me gram was safe, i closed my eyes. i cannot say how long i slept, how long they stayed. but every time i woke, i saw someone there who loved me. manny, tilda, joey, bear.

then someone else crept in. into my dreams he came, stood beside me. stroked my hand. i kept my eyes squeezed shut because i knew he wasn't real. couldn't be. then he whispered in my ear, 'it's okay, birdie, papa's here.'

i sat up. flung myself into his arms.

'papa! papa! oh papa!' and all the cold dammed up inside, all my freezing floodwaters flowed out and out and out.

and afterwards, it took us only minutes to reach gram's room. but already she was far away. angel nectar falling from on high, drip, dripping in her arm. far-off summer breezing gently through her mask. it wasn't just her lungs. the cut the toolbox left was small. but blood had blossomed like a

259

rose inside her head. gently papa told me there was no cure for gram.

we learnt that we were not forsaken, me and joey. nightingale business suddenly became the business of others. but that was okay. tilda's dad knew what to do to get an old man out of jail. compassionate leave to visit his wife in hospital. ten days was all they granted papa. i did not ask, why ten? is that how long it takes, to get to where gram's going? neither papa nor the nurses would have known. the best that we could hope for was the journey would be short.

mr cassidy was not the only one to help us. manny's kind louisa james and bull had offered us a place to stay. papa and joey, me and bear. an apartment that they owned. just down the street from them. with a garden out the back and a bus stop in the front.

louisa cooked for us. sent manny down with soups and sweets and casseroles. so that papa, me and joey could spend as much time as we liked with gram. sometimes we went together. sometimes we visited alone. i tried to keep my feelings separate. the joy of papa's presence. the sadness of gram's absence. the fear that when ten days had passed, i would lose them both.

there was nothing at the hospital for me to do. someone else brushed gram's hair, changed her undies and her nighty.

smoothed ointment on her lips. while i watched gram sleep, i talked to her. reminded her of little things and happy days i thought she might enjoy. like the time we'd laughed about her chest. there were other things i couldn't speak of. these i wrote in letters and left them folded on gram's bed. hoping she might wake and find them when i'd gone.

on the second day, i took inks and pens and pages with me. sketched gram while she was sleeping. drew her world all around her: papa and the garden. plum trees. beans and birds and butterflies and bees. clipped it to her charts when i was leaving. looked back from the door and read what i had written underneath.

this is my gram

she is glorious

please be kind to her while i'm not here.

on the fourth day i went alone again and wrote:

can't talk about the 'd' word, gram. tried to write about it once or twice. then crossed it out again. wish i could do that in real life. cross out the 'd' word. love alice.

i folded the paper into an origami heart. left it on her tea tray.

day six.

i'm worried about papa, gram. not that he's said any-thing, but i think he blames himself for a lot of stuff that's happened. like how you've had to look after me and joey by yourself. how there was no one to look after you, when you got sick. it would be good if you could bring yourself to tell him it's okay. i know you probably can't talk much, even if you were awake. the nurse told papa that there's water in your lungs. they didn't say how it got there. maybe from the flood or from all the times you wanted to cry, but couldn't because you had to look after us. anyhow, if you could just squeeze papa's hand sometime. even once, i think he'd know exactly what you meant. love alice.

on the seventh day i wrote:

  just wanted to tell you that i'm sorry for all the times that i was mean to you. i love you gram. alice

day eight.

  you did a great job, gram. i'm going to be fine. but i'll miss you. love alice.

i didn't want to wake up on the ninth day. i stayed in bed with bear till joey came. he knocked on the door. pushed it open, smiling. hands behind his back, hiding something.

  'ta da!' he magicked a flourish of tulips. yellow as a duck's bill.

  'for gram?' i asked. he shook his head.

  'for you!' he said and put them in my arms.

  'from you?'

  'nope!'

'manny?'

'if they were from manny, he would have brought them himself!' he teased.

'who then?'

'you'll never guess. it was hamish o'leary's mother. she came to the door. i didn't know if you'd want to see her, so i said you were still asleep.'

joey sat down on my bed. suddenly serious. took his time to speak.

'she told me what happened at the house, birdie. i can't believe how brave you were. how brave you've always been.'

he put his arms around me. but not before i'd seen his eyes fill up.

'i just wish gram knew what you did. she'd be so proud of you,' he said.

i lifted up the blankets and we cuddled up in bed till joey needed cheese and pickle sandwiches and bear needed to pee.

'where's papa?' i asked.

'he left early. wants to spend as much time with gram as he can today.'

when the sandwiches were eaten, joey said, 'how about you and me go to the hospital together? and afterwards i'll take you to see manny. he misses you.'

and i missed manny. but i couldn't figure out how to be happy and sad at the same time. how to be – at all. i looked

263

at the pointed yellow buds. fiddled with the thank-you card, the thin green ribbon around the stems.

'it's the ninth day,' i said. in case he hadn't noticed.

'i know,' he said. 'but we never had a chance to say goodbye before. not when our father died, not when our mother left. this time it's different, birdie. it's hard...and i'm scared, but you're the bravest person that i know. please come with me.'

when we arrived, gram was holding papa's hand.

after words

gram's journey ended on the eleventh day.

two weeks later, papa was granted parole. he spends most of his days down on oktober bend. on the river flats where our old home used to be. on tuesdays and on thursdays he teaches boys who've been in trouble with the police how to grow things. together they're making a garden out of mud and sun and seeds.

i wrote to my mother. thought she should know about gram and the flood. about papa and the garden. so far i have received no reply.

manny has made me a website where people can look at my lures and labels and order them. hattie fox at the post office is busy sending them all over the world. 'you must take after your mother, alice nightingale. so talented,' she says. 'you mustn't let anyone stop you.' and i look into her ice-blue eyes and think of gram. of all she gave up for me and joey.

bull says i have already moved mountains, but next

summer i'll face another challenge. i am leaving oktober bend. manny and louisa helped me collect a folio of my drawings. sent them to an art school in the city. the people there offered me a scholarship. granted bear permission to come with me.

papa is a little nervous about my leaving. but i tell him, it's okay, the school is not as far as the 49th parallel. just a train ride away. and i'll be home at weekends. and anyway, no matter what happens, i am the girl who loves the stars at oktober bend. always will be.

from the author

The idea that started me on *The Stars at Oktober Bend* was gleaned from a newspaper article about a homeless girl who sang, and in doing so earned a scholarship to study music at a prestigious conservatorium. I began writing with the intention of telling the story of a girl who sang as a means of escaping a tragic past. But as usually happens, the story became more complex once the character began to evolve and other information came to hand. My daughter was studying for her Masters in Speech Pathology at the time, and I became aware of language disorders, their causes and effects, and this information impacted on my story.

Initially I wrote in the third person, but felt like an observer. So I rewrote it all in first person. Giving Alice a voice empowered me to use a means of expression unique to her. And although her syntax was somewhat unfamiliar, especially in the early stages of the novel, that was when my writing began to flow. Alice thinks of her writing as a means to freedom beyond her circumstances – to flying. 'Words, caught me by surprise,' she says, 'took me in their rushing updraught, took me from the page into the clear mid-air.' That is what recording Alice's thoughts felt like to me – a breathless leave-taking of all that was known and familiar.

about the author

GLENDA MILLARD is a highly respected Australian author who deserves to be better known outside her homeland. Her novel *A Small Free Kiss in the Dark* was the Winner of the 2009 Queensland Premier's Award for young adults, Honour Book in the 2010 CBCA awards for older readers, shortlisted for the 2010 NSW Premier's Literary Awards, and included on the Honour List for the 2012 International Board of Books for Young People. Books from her popular Kingdom of Silk series have also received individual awards. Her novel, *The Novice*, was chosen for a White Raven Award in 2006. Glenda has also written many picture books, including *The Duck and the Darklings*, illustrated by Stephen Michael King. In the UK, *The Stars at Oktober Bend* has been nominated for the CILIP Carnegie Award 2017 and long-listed for the UKLA Awards 2017.

glendamillard.com

A NOTE FROM THE PUBLISHER

Sad things happen in this book, but you will find yourself willing on Alice and Manny as they rejoice in the beauty of the world and work out how to take their places in it. Their story confronts identity and belonging and demonstrates the power of love, family and friendship.

More information about Glenda and *Stars*:

Zoe Toft conducted an extensive interview with Glenda here: *http://www.playingbythebook.net/2016/09/22/stories-were-like-eating-sleeping-breathing-an-interview-with-glenda-millard/*

The YA Fictionados posted an interview with Glenda on YouTube at *https://youtu.be/Bm88ixgc1e8*

We Sat Down blogged about Stars and posted their interview with Glenda here: *http://wesatdown.blogspot.co.uk/2016/11/we-sat-down-for-chatwith-glenda-millard.html*

Teacher's Notes are available at *www.oldbarnbooks.com*

A SMALL FREE KISS IN THE DARK
To be republished in 2017
by Old Barn Books Ltd

ISBN: 978 1 910646 23 6

still alice.
no more.
no less.